WHISPERS OF THE DEVIL

DESIRED BY THE DEVIL
BOOK ONE

BELLA MOONDRAGON

For Amber

CONTENTS

1

LAYLA

THERE ISN'T MUCH that can scare me. Maybe that's why I became a nurse.

Maybe that's why I didn't balk at the idea of spending a summer in an entirely creepy, and no doubt haunted, French Colonial style mansion smack dab in the center of a swamp, cypress lined property in Hahnville, Louisiana.

I've seen scarier places. I've walked the haunted halls of hospitals all over the country during my four years of being a travel nurse. I've seen things in emergency rooms that would make someone's nightmares look and sound like child's play.

This place doesn't scare me. Although, *maybe it should.*

Mom's voice rattles in my ear as she pleads, "Layla, seriously, you can turn around and come home!"

"I already signed the paperwork," I say with a sigh, narrowing my eyes at the gargantuan structure looming in the distant haze of summer.

Overhead, cypress trees hang with vines that dust the top of my

Toyota 4-Runner, the only major purchase I've ever made in my life. Before this moment, I'd been sleeping in bunk beds or on couches in whatever cramped apartments I could find during my nursing rotations. I've never stayed in one place very long. Not long enough to need a car, or to sign for my own apartment, that's for sure. The winding driveway is several miles long by my estimation, guarded by a rotting iron gate covered in vines. The columns on either side were cloaked in wisteria, a stunning purple against the age and decay that seems to ooze from this place like a festering wound.

This place is rotting, like whatever lurks inside the boundary of this property should have been dead a long, long time ago.

"She's *bat-shit crazy*, Layla. There's a reason the rest of the family keeps their distance." Speaking of something that should have died a long time ago, at least in my mom's opinion. "Your great-aunt has been a raving lunatic since she was sixteen."

"Well, I'll be the judge of that, given that I've never met her and only have your exaggerated family stories to back up those claims."

Mom huffs, her voice cracking down the line as the connection shudders. I have one bar of service out here. Maybe that's a good thing, given that my mom has it in mind to call me repeatedly now that she knows of my intentions here. "She's been cooped up in the house for decades, sweetie. I'm talking fifty or sixty years. The place is sinking, you know. Falling into the swamp. Your uncle wanted it condemned back in the eighties, but she flat out refused to leave, and there's nothing that can be done."

"I'm not here to save the house," I argue as my car bumps along the desperately cracked concrete driveway. Cypress roots have sprung from the cement, fanning out like dark claws that dig into the stone like talons. "I'm here because she needs a new night nurse, and the executor of her estate reached out to *me* directly."

"He never said you needed to be the one to bring your life to a grinding halt to make sure she doesn't asphyxiate in her sleep, for Christ's sake!"

I grind my teeth and stare out of the windshield as the house bounds into view, it's once white paint now gray and peeling. Four stories of darkened windows greet me as I pull into the driveway beside a rusted out sedan. "Look, I'm here. I'm fine, okay? I needed a break from the emergency room setting, and this is only a short-term gig. Once a permanent night nurse has been found, I'll be back in Washington, and I'll find another job close by this time."

Mom isn't happy. I imagine her stalking back and forth in front of the bay window in my old childhood home in Kirkland, Washington, just outside of Seattle. "There's a reason no one goes there, Layla."

"Because it's haunted?" I laugh, leaning my head back against the headrest and letting my car idle. "I should tell you about some of the stuff I've seen in emergency rooms, Mom."

Whatever she says next crackles with static, the line breaking up, and then the call drops.

It's for the best, I think. Mom has been trying to talk me out of this since the day I told her I'd been contacted by a lawyer in New Orleans whose practice has my great-aunt Penny as a client.

I've never met my aunt. All I know is that she never married, is childless, and is the heir to the family estate that dates back to the early 1800s. This place used to be a plantation, which is sordid enough, but add in the family lore about this particular line....

My fingertips tingle as I slowly get out of the car and shut the door, shielding my eyes from the sun as I look up at the windows. The screened-in front porch rattles as someone opens an interior door, and then a petite dark-haired woman peeks her head around the screen door. She holds it open, a beautiful, kind smile touching her lips. "You must be Layla Bryant!"

Her thick creole accent immediately calms my nerves. I smile back at her, saying, "Yeah, that's me. I'm glad I'm in the right place. It took ages to get here after passing the gate."

"There's a faster way off the property." She glances at my car. "Especially if you have four-wheel drive. It's a dirt road that connects with the neighbor's property. Come on in, it's stifling today. I just made iced tea. You thirsty?" Her golden-brown skin glistens in the unforgiving sunlight as she clutches the screen door.

I am thirsty. Hot, sweaty, and absolutely parched. I nod and walk to the trunk of my car. I hike my duffle bag over my shoulder–all that I have in the world besides my car.

"I'm Bailey Elliott, by the way," she says from the porch.

"It's nice to meet you, Bailey. Are you Penny Gregory's day nurse, then?"

"I am." Her smile is bright, all of her teeth shining white in the sunlight.

I glance up at the balconies and windows one last time before we go inside, and for a moment, I think I see a figure standing at one of the third floor windows. The shadow moves away just as a cloud stretches overhead, blocking some of the light. *Strange*, I tell myself as I walk up a set of steps and follow Bailey across the porch. I'm used to shadows in strange places, but the second I enter the house, I get that creeping sensation I normally feel while working alone at night in the hospital. It's like I'm being watched from afar by something desperate and curious, something that isn't sure it wants to be seen. Not yet, at least.

"I can see the family resemblance," Bailey says over her shoulder as she shuts the front door behind us. Her steps cause the wood floor to creak until she reaches a weathered, ornate rug situated in front of a wide, aging staircase.

I blink at her, tucking a lock of my golden blonde hair behind my ear. "Really? Honestly, I've never met my great-aunt. My family is all spread out now, all over the country."

"You have the Gregory eyes," Bailey says while motioning toward my face. "There's a bunch of portraits on the second floor, in the hallway that leads to the cigar room. You'll see. Every one of those people have those big blue eyes and that pointed chin. You look like Ms. Penny, actually. There's a portrait of her in the library. When I saw you get out of your car, I about had a heart attack thinking Ms. Penny had somehow escaped and come back sixty years younger."

Bailey's soft laugh is like music, but I stand awkwardly in the foyer and look around. It's clean, but there's still an underlying layer of decay hanging in the air. Mom might have been right about this place.

It feels like I'm standing in another era, like this house has simply been lost to time.

Through an archway to my left, a formal sitting room comes into view. A jet-black grand piano has been waxed so thoroughly the sunlight gleams off it, spreading rays of light all over the faded chaise lounges and dust covered antique tables.

Bailey follows me as I turn to look deeper into the room. "The formal dining room is just through that archway there, and beyond that is the kitchen, which wraps around the backside of the house. There's a few smaller rooms back there too. Laundry room, two small bunk rooms, which I think used to be the house servants' quarters way back in the day." She walks back into the foyer. "On the right side, there's another sitting room in the back, a sunroom. It gets awfully hot in there this time of year, though. And this–" she walks through the second archway leading off the foyer, her hands spread wide, "this is where we keep all of Ms. Penny's supplies, you see. It might've been an office at one point."

Metal shelves that look so out of place are covered in white boxes full of medicine and other supplies–gauze, syringes, tubes and latex gloves. The sterile smell immediately brings me back to the hospitals I've spent so much time in, and I shiver with a sudden uneasy feeling that brushes over my skin, causing the fine, downy hair on my arms to stand on end.

Bailey leads me through the first floor of the house. It's a maze of doors and snug hallways leading to the kitchen. Sunlight streams through the back windows as she pours iced tea and hands me a glass, which is cold to the touch. It's a welcome relief from the unrelenting heat.

"There's no AC right now, but we keep the windows open in the summer to let the breeze in. It seems to help, and Ms. Penny doesn't seem to mind the heat."

"We?"

"Well," she says, smacking her lips. "There's me, the day nurse. I'm here Monday through Friday until around five and occasionally on Saturdays. Vera works on the weekends and on-call if I need a hand.

She's an old, gnarled crone, that woman. I don't like her all that much." She sips from her tea, her dark curls dancing with the motion. "And then there's Curtis. He's our handyman. He's been fighting with the AC all spring to no avail, but you'll see him around nonetheless. He comes out once a week to tidy up the landscaping out front and back and checks on the house. He loves those gardens out there. His family goes way, way back with the Gregorys, you see." She leans her hip against the kitchen counter, which is a pale green and made of vinyl. Everything in the kitchen is dated, like it hasn't been renovated since the 1960s, at least.

Bailey continues, "Ms. Penny is… far gone, I'm afraid. A lot of what Vera and I do is just maintenance–keeping her comfortable. She doesn't eat much anymore and has an IV for fluids if she doesn't drink much during the day. She doesn't talk to us these days, not that she did much of that anyway. She talks to herself sometimes though. You might hear her from time to time."

I nod along, my eyes fixated on the thick cypress grove encircling the house. In the distance, against the swaying vines and leaping insects, I can see still water glistening against a group of scattered headstones.

"That's the family cemetery," Bailey says with a sigh. "The swamp is… getting closer to the house, you know. The foundation is all muddled and sinking in spots. I've been told the house is perfectly safe, but because of the way it's settling, you might hear some strange noises at night. The pipes are pretty loud, and sometimes it even sounds like a freight train is coming right through the center of the house if someone runs the washing machine. It just has old bones, you see. Like Ms. Penny."

"Is it haunted?" It's a silly question, but I can't help myself, especially while my gaze stays locked on the cemetery in the distance.

Bailey chuckles, but there's no real laughter in the sound. "Mmm… that depends on who you ask. This place is old, but you know that, being family and all."

In truth, I don't know much. All I know is that my great-great aunt and uncle, Aunt Penny's parents, had only one child, Penny. Her father's siblings left the family estate and spread out, creating the family lines I belonged to. I knew her father had died young, and her mother, based on family lore, went clinically insane after his death and died in an asylum in the early '60s. In reality, Penny Gregory is more of a distant cousin, but every time my mom brought her up, it was always aunt this, and aunt that, so I've always thought of her as my great-aunt.

Aunt Penny is the last of the Gregory line, the prolific name dying with her when that time came.

"Why did the last night nurse quit?" I ask, turning to face Bailey.

She takes a sip from her iced tea and looks absently out the window, shrugging. "She didn't like being here at night, which kind of defeats the purpose of her employment, doesn't it?"

"I guess it does," I laugh, shaking my head.

"I should probably show you where to put your things, huh? I'll try to give you a tour of the rest of the house before I leave this evening, but it's a big place. I haven't even seen half the rooms myself, and I've been here for three years. I live in Hahnville, so I don't stay here, but I swear the bedrooms are perfectly comfortable."

Bailey leads me upstairs, which is dark and foreboding. The floors creak painfully with each step as the long, darkened hallway she leads me down seems to narrow and twist, the floor slightly angled and off kilter.

"This is you." She smiles, opening a door toward the back of the house. The room is warm but faces north, putting it out of the glare of the sun. It smells sharply of wisteria, lilac, and fresh laundry, which is a welcome relief from the dusty smell in the lower level of the house. The linens are a calming white color, and the walls bleed with hand-painted floral wallpaper that doesn't show a single sign of its age.

Even the bathroom, with its antique finishes, looks new, or at least renovated.

"Ms. Penny's rooms are just across the hall," Bailey says, planting her hands on her hips. "I guess I should introduce the two of you. What do you say?"

2

LAYLA

AUNT PENNY COULD BE MISTAKEN for a child from a distance. The top of her silver hair barely reaches my sternum as she rests in her bed, and I'm not a tall woman, by any means. She's definitely not the withered old crone I expected, not with her dainty, childlike features and huge, blue eyes.

I've never even seen a picture of her before. In truth, I could count on one hand the number of times her name had been brought up in conversation.

I'm not sure what I imagined her to look like. All I had to go off were stories about this place and this specific family line. But her brow isn't perpetually pinched. Her nose isn't long and gnarled and covered with warts. Her fingernails can't scratch my eyes out, and I doubt she had a cauldron hidden somewhere in the house where she boiled potions.

She doesn't look like the witch my family made her out to be.

It makes me sad, honestly, seeing her lying motionless in the massive four-poster bed. It swallows her tiny body whole, making her look like a discarded porcelain doll. Her white nightdress is absolutely pristine, her nails freshly manicured, and her hair is pinned in rollers like she has big plans tomorrow and wants to look her best.

In reality, Bailey takes exceptional care of her, and that's all there is to it.

I spend the next few days shadowing her and Vera, the on-call nurse. Vera has been with Aunt Penny for decades now, and while she rarely speaks a word to me during the handful of nights I watch her care for my aunt, I pick up a lot from the elderly nurse.

Night care, it seems, is simply just… being here.

I gently tuck the sheets around my aunt's frail body, smiling up into her glassy blue eyes. It's just after 1:00 in the morning, but Aunt Penny shows no signs that she's tired. In fact, I don't think I've even seen her blink in the past hour, but her chest moves with each calm, steady breath, and the ECG next to the bed is full of green lines, the device quiet, save for the soft thump monitoring her heartbeat.

She suffered a stroke a few months ago, and while she's somewhat recovered, I can tell whatever consciousness is there isn't enough for her to live a full life anymore. It's heartbreaking.

"It's rather warm in here," I say to her, wiping the back of my hand over my forehead. A soft, rain-soaked breeze drifts in from the open window, a screen keeping the insects at bay. I hate to close the window, but the rain is picking up, so I do.

She says nothing, her eyes fixed on a far corner of the darkened room. I check my watch and sigh as I carefully meet her eyes again, then start going through the checklist Vera gave me. It's nearly 2:00 in the morning when I finally gather my supplies and begin to leave the room.

"Amos," Aunt Penny says behind me, her voice a faint whisper against the breeze.

For a moment, I think I've imagined it, but she says it again, much softer this time. Her heart monitor picks up an arrhythmia, which causes me to abruptly turn around and watch the monitor with interest. "Aunt Penny?" I say into the dark. "Are you all right?"

I walk toward the bed, my gaze sliding from the monitor to my aunt, who has moved for the first time since I started tending to her at night by myself. Her long, thin fingers curl over the sheets as she takes a ragged breath. "Amos–"

But the moment is over before I can blink. She takes a deep breath, her eyes fluttering closed as the monitor resumes its rhythmic, steady beeping.

"Amos," I whisper, shrugging, a wistful smile tugging at the corner of my mouth. "Sounds romantic. Did you have a lover once, Aunt Penny?"

My only answer is the beeping of her monitor.

I stand there for a moment watching to make sure she's not having an attack of any kind then leave the room as I'd intended, realizing I've been holding my breath. I let it out in a whoosh as I close her bedroom door behind me.

The hallway is dark, no moonlight to guide my way while I walk to the staircase. I've gotten used to clicks, creaks, and occasionally thumping banging sounds the house makes at night and usually don't bother to turn on a light. I've noticed the noises get worse if it rains, or if the humidity is especially suffocating. What had Bailey said to me when I first came here?

The house has old bones, just like Ms. Penny.

I remind myself that this place doesn't scare me as I creep downstairs to put away the supplies I'd gathered for the nightly ritual of putting my aunt to bed. Her thin skin doesn't tolerate an IV for very long, and a lot of my night is spent tending to superficial wounds and making sure she's comfortable, and her vitals are strong.

I put my unused supplies away and safely discard any sharps. The house around me is still, near silent, while outside a storm brews in the distance. It's been sprinkling on and off for hours, but now it rains in earnest as I begin to walk back upstairs and start getting ready for bed.

Thunder rattles the house as I walk into the foyer. A soft rattle ripples all around me, like the thunder is strong enough to disturb the old paintings now trembling in their frames. I think nothing of it, my foot on the first step heading upstairs, when a loud scraping sound echoes from the formal living room, followed by sudden, crackling of jazz music.

I slowly edge toward the living room. There's an old gramophone in the corner of the room–spinning, it's needle skipping and scratching against a record.

"Folks', I'm goin' down to St. James Infirmary, see my baby there–" The record skips, the voice of the singer distorted and cracking. *"She's stretched out on a long, white table. So sweet, so cold, so fair–"*

The record screeches. It's a horrible sound that makes my ears ring as I edge closer to the gramophone.

"Let her go, let her go, God bless her ohh! Wherever she may be. She can search this wide world over. She'll never find another sweet man like me–"

I pull the needle from the record and the song, "St. James Infirmary" by Cab Calloway, cuts out abruptly.

Silence settles over the room again, penetrated by the thundering rain. The hair on the back of my neck rises as I tear my gaze from the record and look over my shoulder into the inky black shadows choking the room around me. I'm alone, but I have the odd sense that someone is watching me as I leave the living room and head upstairs to my room.

I check Aunt Penny's ECG stats on the tablet I share with Bailey, which is set up to alert me with an alarm if anything goes wrong during the night, before undressing and stepping into the shower, letting the lukewarm water thaw my senses. Normally, my showers would be scalding, but not in this unforgiving humidity.

I run my fingers through my thick blonde hair and scrub hard, washing the day away. Even with the heat, humidity, bugs, and creepy haunted gramophones, this place isn't so bad after all. My suite, anyway, is a dream compared to some of the places where I've had to stay before. My bathroom is stocked with luxurious products, a far cry from the drugstore shampoo and conditioner I picked up on my way here. The conditioner I work into my hair smells like honeysuckle and vanilla, a warm, clean scent that makes me close my eyes and breathe deeply.

Another scent wraps itself around me in an embrace that slightly blurs my senses. It's something... musky, dark, and delicious. A male fragrance, through and through. Like leather, smoke, and sweat. I lean my head against the shower wall and breathe deeply, letting the scent flood my system while the cool water flows over my bare breasts and stomach, igniting a spark deep in my belly where warmth begins to bloom.

Shit, I'm turned on. And by what? Expensive shampoo?

I smile to myself, chuckling as I raise my face to the shower head.

The feeling lingers, however, while I lie in bed listening to the house groan against the thundering rain. My hands drift between my legs, my skin still cool and damp from the shower. I close my eyes and let my knees fall to the side as my fingers glide over my inner thighs and back up again to cup my breasts.

Admittedly, it's been over a year since I've had sex. At least, from what I can remember, it's been that long. Sure, I've messed around, but being a travel nurse hadn't worked in my favor when it came to anything more than the occasional hookup that left me feeling gross and wholly unsatisfied.

Thinking of the few encounters I had during my last gig, which included a resident in a supply closet during an especially long night shift, makes that ache between my legs evaporate in a single second, and I let my hands fall to my sides.

I don't know when I actually fell asleep. The room fades back into view, and for a moment I wonder if I'm still asleep when I feel the bed shift like someone is climbing on top of it.

There's that thick, heady scent again. All male. Sweat and desire. I taste whiskey on his lips as his tongue sweeps over mine.

He sucks my neck as his kisses trail down between my legs.

I'm dreaming. This is a dream. This is just a dream.

I look up at the ceiling, my hand tangling in his hair—thick, soft curls that feel divine when I run my fingers through it and tug ever so slightly. His teeth graze my inner thighs, his tongue lashing out and dragging over my skin as he kisses up, then his tongue parts my folds, adding new life to the desperate ache between my legs.

I arch off the bed, but his arm comes down on my waist, pinning me in place. He's rough, starving, like my taste on his tongue is a feast, and he can't control himself. He sucks my clit and pumps his fingers inside me—each thrust rough and demanding, his fingers curling and pulling me closer to the edge of the pleasure I'd given up on just a few hours ago. The song I heard earlier starts up again, a rhythmic groan in the background. *"So sweet, so cold, so fair..."*

This is a dream. You're asleep.

I cry out, my voice piercing the air as my body begins to shake. "Please, *please!*" *More.* I need so much more.

A low laugh echoes around me. The stranger from my darkest, wildest dreams presses a kiss to my clit. "Beg for it."

I come undone, losing control entirely. Another lick, and I'm gritting my teeth to stop myself from screaming loud enough to shatter the windows. Pleasure floods my body, rocking through me in waves. I've never felt anything so strong before in my life.

I open my eyes with a start to daylight flooding the room. I tear my hand from between my thighs, panting, sweat dripping down my face as I squint into the sunlight pouring through the windows.

I feel an odd sense that I'm not alone as I look around the room, narrowing my eyes into the dusty haze of golden sun now warming my bed.

Just a dream. Just a really, *really* sexy dream. I let out my breath and close my eyes. My body feels electric, still begging to be touched, and touched by whoever that stranger had been in my dream.

"You're losing it," I whisper, gripping the sheets.

Just then, my alarm goes off. I have a habit of waking up a few minutes before my alarm, and honestly, I don't feel like I've gotten any sleep at all. I slowly swing my legs out of bed and then stop.

Soft, red bruises line the inside of my thighs. I suck in a breath, holding it, closing my eyes as I try to calm the sudden pitch in my heart rate.

Just a dream, I tell myself again. I did that to myself, which fills me with nothing but embarrassment. Maybe my nursing friends were right about getting laid. It'd been far too long, and now look at me?

I've peppered myself with bruises in my sleep having a wet dream like a sex-crazed teenage boy going through puberty.

I quickly get out of bed and pull on a T-shirt and shorts, ignoring the sets of scrubs I brought here with me, at least for today. My skin prickles. I brush my hair and pull it back in a ponytail as I look at my reflection in the mirror. My cheeks burn. I can barely meet my own eyes.

Why do I feel so violated if I've done this to myself?

I shove the thought aside and tear out of the room, barefoot, ready to tackle the next hour or so of my morning duties before Bailey gets here to take over. But I've barely made it down the hallway to my aunt's room when I hear what I think is a door slamming shut overhead. I freeze. "Bailey?"

A tremor groans through the ceiling above me.

I slowly turn to the staircase at the far end of the hallway that leads to the third and fourth floors, which are nothing but bedrooms and storage rooms. I haven't spent much time up there at all.

"Hello?" I say, my voice cracking over the word. Silence. Pure, creeping silence that settles in my bones and causes my hair to stand on end.

I nearly jump out of my skin when the front door opens, setting another shutter through the house.

"Bailey," I breathe, loud enough she hears me.

"I know I'm early!" Bailey's sing-song voice drifts up the stairs to the second floor as I walk to the landing and look down. She holds up two iced lattes, shaking them slightly. "I thought we'd celebrate your first night working alone in the house."

My heart is pounding as I nod, swallowing hard.

"Are you okay?" she asks, her brow furrowing. "I scared you, didn't I?"

I bite my lip and resist the urge to look back down the hallway toward the second flight of stairs.

Why do I feel like there's someone–or something–standing there, right now, watching me?

"I bought croissants too." Bailey grins, but the smile doesn't reach her eyes.

3

Layla

Bailey dumps an assortment of pastries on a serving platter in the humid, sun drenched kitchen. I lean on the counter and take a sip of my iced latte, praying the caffeine will hit my system and thaw the numbness still gripping my body.

Whatever happened earlier this morning still has me in somewhat of a trance. I can't shake the feeling I hadn't been alone in that upstairs hallway, and especially that I hadn't been alone in my room.

"You're holding that coffee like it's a weapon." Bailey giggles, rolling her eyes as she picks up the platter and sets it on the kitchen table. "Are you okay?"

"I didn't sleep well at all," I admit, blinking into the unforgiving sunlight. God, it's hot. It's not even 8:00 in the morning. and the entire room is already suffocating with heat. I press the plastic cup to my temple and sigh with relief.

Bailey watches me curiously for a moment then shrugs. "You should go get some rest, then. You're the night nurse, remember? You should really be getting ready for bed right now."

"It was a quiet night," I tell her, the cold coffee easing the pounding in my skull. "I went to bed around two, I think. No alarms at all last night."

"Well, don't get used to it. Ms. Penny's mostly active at night lately. It's the dementia, you know."

I nod. I do know that. I also know that Bailey's right, and I should be upstairs and back in bed, but the thought of being alone right now has my chest tightening and my fingers prickling with adrenaline. "Is the house haunted?" It's not the first time I've asked her.

Bailey sinks into a chair with a sigh, her normally sunny expression fading. "I don't think so, but you never know with these old houses." She waves a hand around the room. "Why? Did the pipes keep you up last night?"

"Maybe." I sit down across from her, my body aching with sudden fatigue. "I'm not really sure what happened. I thought I heard–"

"Hello? Anybody home?" A rich, male voice echoes from the front foyer.

Bailey rises, a smile brushing over her mouth as she catches my eye. "It's just the pipes groaning Layla, I swear."

"Who is that?" I ask, standing.

"Oh, that'll be the neighbors. I'm sure they're here to meet you. Real nice couple, I promise. Come on." She takes my hand and practically drags me through the narrow hallway toward the foyer.

A middle aged couple stands in the center of the entryway surrounded by brown paper bags full of groceries. The woman, dressed in a flattering pink floral sundress, beams at us as she turns, a basket full of produce in her hands. "My, my, look at you!" Her neatly curled brown hair bounces on her shoulders as she steps forward, extending the basket in my direction.

The man takes the heavy basket from the woman and gives her a soft, knowing smile. "You haven't even introduced yourself, Helen. Now you're forcing vegetables on the poor young woman."

"I'm getting ahead of myself." She laughs. "I'm Helen Wilson, and this is my husband Robert. We live just down the road, your closest neighbors."

"Oh," I say, giving them a polite smile. "I'm Layla."

"Well, of course you are, dear! Just look at you. You're a Gregory, through and through."

I blush deeply and smile, bobbing my head in thanks. Bailey gives me a knowing look before stepping forward to accept the basket of produce from Robert. "You didn't have to drive over. I could have picked all of this up myself."

"Well, Robert here saw your grocery order, and we decided to come pay you a visit," Helen cuts in, her light brown eyes creasing as she glances from Bailey to me. "Robert owns the grocery store in town, my dear. If you ever need anything, you just let us know."

"Their number is hanging on the fridge already," Bailey says with a teasing smile. "You just wanted to come over and see the new nurse, didn't you?"

Robert chuckles, but Helen looks playfully stricken. "Helen here has been in a fit about it since we found out the news last Sunday at church. Everyone in town is talking about it."

"Talking about what?" I ask, some of my earlier unease slipping back into place.

"You, of course," Helen says with a little wave of her hand. "Now, I didn't believe it myself when Thomas Hart came to the eleven o'clock service last Sunday and said he had a new nurse coming to the Gregory Estate. We pray over Ms. Penny, regularly, you see, which is why he told us. He'd been calling around for weeks looking for a nurse, calling all the big hospitals. You name it, he called it." Helen chuckles, beaming up at her husband. "And then, by some miracle, he found you. A descendent, no less. I couldn't believe it. None of us believed he'd actually had Ms. Penny's distant cousin coming back to the Gregory estate. We thought this place would fall into the marsh eventually."

"Oh, I'm–" I clear my throat, planting a polite smile back on my face. "I'm not here because I'm hoping to inherit the estate, not by any means."

Robert and Helen give me a curious look, but at that same

moment, Bailey's watch begins to beep. "I'd better get Ms. Penny her morning medicine. It was so nice seeing you both!"

"You too, Bailey. I'll see you on Sunday." Helen gives Bailey a motherly look of disapproval while Bailey rolls her eyes. "Your mama promised me you'd start coming back to church when you didn't have to work on the weekends here anymore."

"I'll be there on Sunday." Bailey forces a laugh, waving goodbye before turning toward the stairs and walking out of sight.

I stand in the foyer with the Wilsons, unsure of what to say, or do. "Uh, thank you so much for the groceries. I better put everything away before things start to melt."

Helen scoffs, shaking her head. "Let us help you, dear. You're probably exhausted from being up all night."

I pick up a few of the bags, which are rather heavy, and balance them on my hips. Now I know who to thank for all the luxurious bath products. "Aunt Penny is actually pretty easy going at night–"

"Oh, no," Helen says in a low tone as we follow Robert, who is carrying the rest of the groceries in his burly arms, down the narrow hallway toward the kitchen. "I'm talking about the house."

I pause mid-step, turning to face her. "Wh-what do you mean?"

She eyes me curiously, searching for something behind my eyes. "It's nothing, dear. These old homes… well, they make a lot of noise, and it's a different kind of dark when the sun goes down, you know?"

Something in her eyes tells me there's a lot more she wants to say, but Robert calls out to us from the kitchen. "Better bring me those groceries, miss. Your bags have the eggs and ice cream in them."

I reluctantly tear my gaze away from Helen and ignore the creeping sensation licking up my spine as I hurry to the kitchen, handing Robert the bags. "I really could have done all this myself. It would've given me something to do today–"

"Oh, it's no bother. I'm sure you have your hands entirely too full with Ms. Penny's care. Plus, I have been meaning to check out the dining room for some time and always forget when I'm over dropping things off."

"The dining room?" I ask as he closes the freezer and turns to face me. "What about the dining room?" But Robert is already stepping past me.

He walks through the narrow kitchen and opens the door leading directly into the formal dining room, which I haven't spent a single second of time in since arriving.

Sunlight pours into the narrow space, illuminating the antique eight-person mahogany table in ribbons of gold. Compared to other areas of the house, this room has been renovated recently.

"Well, the man did a fine job, if I do say so myself."

"Who?" I ask, watching as Robert narrows his eyes on the intricate floral wallpaper.

"Curtis hired an artist a while back to come here to repaint the wallpaper, to give it new life. Even though it's been a while since he painted this room, it still looks fresh. I will say I was nervous about it. The Historical Society has been gunning to make the Gregory Estate a protected property for years now, and having someone come in and rip up the place didn't sit well with me, but... looks like the guy just brought the wallpaper back to life, is all."

"It must have taken that poor man hours to do this," Helen whispers, her eyes wide as she scans the room.

I stare at the wallpaper and wonder what's so damn special about it when Helen turns to me and says, "It's original to the house, if you can believe it. Two hundred year old wallpaper. Isn't it just crazy to think about all the dinners served in this room, all of the family members who looked at this very same wallpaper two centuries ago?"

I swallow hard and nod, that creeping sensation only growing in intensity. "I'm sure the ghosts in the house appreciate keeping it the way it's always been."

Robert's hardy laugh cuts through the air, but Helen isn't laughing. She isn't smiling, either. She just stares at me with an unreadable expression, her lips softly parted like she's trying to find the words to tell me something.

"Well, we best be going. Come on, Helen."

"It was very nice to meet you, Miss Layla," she says, but her voice is strained. She turns to her husband, who is already walking away, cutting through the living room to get back to the front foyer.

But Helen lingers for a moment, wringing her hands.

"Is–is everything all right?" I ask, my mouth going dry.

Helen looks at me over her shoulder and nods, sighing, "These old houses... you never feel entirely alone, do you?"

"No," I reply, giving her a soft smile.

"I meant it when I said that if you ever need anything, just call. We live on the next property over. It's only a ten minute drive. You're welcome anytime, dear. *I mean it.*"

The force behind her words catches me off guard, like a warning has been laced in between each syllable.

I watch her walk away, joining her husband in the foyer. I only catch their shadows stretching across the worn rug before they disappear from sight entirely, lost to the glare of the sun.

Running my hand over my face, I rub the exhaustion from my eyes. I need to sleep. My anxiety and stress, and that creepy, crawly feeling in my stomach.... It's just a lack of sleep, surely. I can feel the fatigue settling into my bones as I make my way upstairs and turn into my room.

No musky, leathery scent this time. Just sunlight and the smell of clean linens.

But the second I lie in bed and close my eyes against the sun, the clunking, creaking noises start up again and blend into what I think are footsteps pacing in front of my door.

I can't tell if I'm dreaming or not.

I should probably get used to it.

4

LAYLA

AUNT PENNY STARES AHEAD, per usual, looking at everything and nothing all at once. I turn a page in the book I've been reading aloud to her the past four nights. She recently started a new blood pressure medication that's supposed to make her feel drowsy, but so far, it's having the opposite effect. The old woman has been staring into space until 3:00 or 4:00 in the morning the past couple of nights, and I'm running out of ways to keep myself busy.

"Don't!" I say in an exaggerated tone, lifting my voice to imitate the dainty, elegant and high-bred young debutant, the book's heroine. "Please! You know we cannot go any further, Randall. You'll ruin me!"

I swear Aunt Penny's mouth lifts into a ghost of a smile, her eyes softening and looking far more alive than they had only moments ago.

I drop my voice as low as it can go and continue, "You called me a rake once, Juliette…. It's high time I showed you just how *rakish* I can be…." I quickly scan the rest of the page and glance up at Aunt Penny, clearing my throat. "I think that's enough of that for the night, Aunt Penny."

She closes her eyes as if in agreement. *Finally.* This poor woman has been up for hours with no relief. I set the book on top of her dresser and stretch, my back which is aching from sitting in an ancient wingback armchair for the last three hours. I walk to her bedside, glancing at the monitor, then turn off her bedside lamp. "I'll talk to Bailey in the morning and see if we can do anything that will help you sleep better, okay?"

My only answer is her quiet, rhythmic breathing.

I smile down at my aunt, taking in the soft lines of her frail face. I can see how she was beautiful once, a real stunner, actually. It makes all of this more heartbreaking. She'd been my age once, twenty-six with nothing but her future ahead of her. But that future had been… this. Rotting away alone in this creepy-ass house.

My sneakers are silent as I cross the hall and walk to my bedroom. It's been quiet in the house lately, which might have to do with the work Curtis has been doing on the new HVAC system, which still isn't working. But tonight feels electric, like a storm is brewing. I can almost taste the rain, and the humidity is thicker than it's been in days.

I pause at my door, remembering I left my water bottle in Aunt Penny's room. I really don't want to risk waking her up, but the thought of walking all the way to the kitchen in the dark….

I chew my lower lip and glance toward the stairwell, the darkness closing in on me with each passing second.

I've been here for two weeks, and I'm still not used to this place. I've gotten over that initial fear, of course, of the darkened corners and bumps in the night. I sleep right through it now, especially since I'm getting used to my aunt's odd sleep schedule and can sleep during the day again without issue.

But again, there's something in the air tonight. Something that tells me I'm not entirely alone here right now.

"I just need a glass of water," I say to the house and the ghosts that surely inhabit it then run like mad down the stairs into the foyer.

I really need to get a grip.

I feel like a scared little girl trying to find my way through the dark to my mom's bedroom as I hug the wall and feel my way to the kitchen. The light switches in this old house are in odd places, and the one in the main hallway is right next to the kitchen door, unfortunately, meaning I have to walk the entire way in pitch black.

By the time I reach the kitchen, the rain starts. The soft evening drizzle gives way to full, thundering sheets that sweep toward the house, splashing against the windows as I enter the kitchen and turn on the light. The back porch light illuminates the rear of the house, giving new life to how hard it's raining right now. I stare out the window over the sink as I fill a glass with water, watching the rain fall in dizzying sheets that are both terrifying and oddly soothing.

The Gulf is only a few miles away, creeping closer and closer every year. The far edge of the Gregory property is now protected marsh land, from what Curtis told me. I spent a whole afternoon sitting on the back porch while he tried to fix the lawnmower, listening to him talk about great blue heron and red knots.

Maybe one of these days I'll explore the grounds a little bit and see for myself what kind of wildlife this place has to offer.

I smile a bit wistfully as I raise my glass to my lips. When was the last time I had time to explore any of the places I've worked at over the last four years? Being here, in my family's ancestral home, gives me the sudden urge to slow down and enjoy myself, to explore, to put down roots for the first time since I left home for college.

A creaking sound directly behind me snaps me out of my head, and I whirl, expecting someone to be standing in the doorway to the kitchen. My heart rate spikes, adrenaline coursing through my veins, but there's no one there.

The fridge kicks on, sending a near silent vibration through the room.

I know better than to start rattling off names. It's almost 5:00 in the morning. Bailey won't be here for a few hours, and Curtis never comes this early, especially when there's a storm circling the property.

Hell, even Vera, who only comes in on the weekends now, won't show her face until 11:00 or 12:00 to start her shift.

I swallow past the lump in my throat and slowly turn back to the sink to rinse my glass. Lightning flashes, illuminating the cypress trees at the edge of the backyard.

My eyes catch on a shadow that hadn't been there before. Just beyond the tree line. I squint, trying to get a better look, but the porch light only stretches so far.

Another flash of lightning lights up the sky. I rear back, my heart leaping into my throat as the blue-hued light illuminates what I am sure is someone standing amidst the trees, looking at the house.

The lightning fades, but the figure moves forward just a step, close enough I can see the outline of the hood shielding their face from view. At least, I think that's what I see.

I feel absolutely out of my body as I wrench open the drawer next to the sink and pull out a knife, gripping the handle so tightly my knuckles turn white. I don't know what I'm thinking when I unlock the backdoor and yank it open so hard it bounces off the wall and nearly slams into me as I step out onto the back porch. "Hey!" I shout, brandishing the knife. "Get out of here!"

The figure doesn't move.

"I-I said get out of here! I'll call the police!"

Nothing.

I'm starting to shake, but I stifle it, keeping my expression grave and determined. I've been attacked by my patients before, nothing serious, but enough to spur me into signing up for self-defense classes at the local gym. Whoever this is, they're standing far enough away that their body is still obstructed by the trees, and the rain isn't helping me get a glimpse of their face, that's for sure. But I could take them, right? I could defend this house, and my aunt, if necessary. "I will call the police!"

Lightning crashes overhead, followed by thunder so violent the house seems to groan in anguish. I step back, startled by the thunder, and blink.

The figure is gone, just like that.

I rush back into the house, locking the door, and run upstairs. The knife is still in my hand when I trip on the last few steps, my knees cracking against the second floor landing. "Fuck!" I hiss, not daring to close my eyes or look behind me. The house rattles against another earth-shaking clap of thunder that splits the sky in two, and I'm up again, running straight to my aunt's room. I lock the door behind me, leaning on it as I take a ragged breath.

She's asleep, her ECG monitor beeping quietly with each steady heartbeat it reads.

I let my breath out slowly, willing my heart to stop pounding, and begin to wonder if I overreacted. I couldn't see shit, for one. Not in the storm. Not in the dark. Not against the tangled cypress trees and overgrown vines that choke the tree line. I'm also tired, my eyes strained from looking at the faded text of a slutty Regency romance book from the early nineties all night.

But it felt so real. Too real.

I sink into the wingback chair, facing the door, and rest the knife on my lap. I wait for what seems like hours, until my eyes grow heavy, and my head begins to nod. I fight it, but I'm pulled into the kind of depthless sleep only true exhaustion can accomplish. Somewhere in the distance, I hear that song again, the smooth jazz a far cry from the aged, crackling notes that came from the gramophone.

"*Layla*," a deep male voice says in my ear. "You fell asleep here again. I should punish you for this." I'm lifted in the air, strong arms cradling me.

"Punish me, then."

I feel my back hit a mattress.

His hands are on my thighs, rough and demanding as his thumbs hook under my shorts, and he pulls them down.

I can taste him on my lips—sweet, spicy, salty—like he's just finished a glass of fine scotch. I suck his lower lip into my mouth, biting down.

He nudges my legs apart, rasping, "You're fucking soaked, Layla. Those filthy books make you wet, don't they?"

I arch my hips as his fingers glide down over my clit, sliding through the wetness pooling between my thighs. "P-please–"

"I love it when you beg," he whispers in my ear then bites down on my neck. He pulls my underwear to the side, and I cry out against the pain then the sudden pressure between my legs. He's enormous, stretching me to the point where it hurts, where I'm not sure I can take him any further.

"What were you doing with this?" he whispers, his voice low and full of gravel as something cool touches the outside of my thigh.

I go rigid, his cock buried inside me.

"Layla," he taunts, running the flat of the knife along my thigh.

I squirm, trying to get away, but he has me pinned.

"Please–"

His mouth lowers over mine as he smooths the knife up and down my thigh, then up again, slicing through my underwear. I take a deep breath as he presses his cock deeper. "Does it hurt?"

"Yes–"

"Good."

Another thrust has me screaming, gripping the sheets as he fucks me hard and fast, using me like a toy. He rises up over me, his face obscured by shadows, and uses the knife to cut through my shirt, tearing it off my body and tossing it across the room as he pumps into me. He slams the knife down into the bed next to me, piercing the mattress. His hands rest on my breasts, squeezing them as he grinds his hips into mine until I'm babbling incoherently, the tension in my lower belly screaming for release.

I'm so close. Each thrust is more brutal than the last, and it's exactly what I need. It's what I'd never admit I'd like–being chased. Being used and dominated. He grips my neck, squeezing.

"Come for me," he says in a loud, stern voice that has me quaking around him. I suck in a desperate, life giving breath….

"Holy fuck!" I peel myself off the floor in my aunt's bedroom, coated in sweat and panting as I squint into the stormy daylight pouring through the curtains. I rise, trembling, my shirt damp with sweat, and a quick glance in the mirror over her dresser reveals my hair is ruffled and my face... entirely flushed.

I creep to the door, glancing at my still sleeping aunt. The door is locked, and suddenly the events of the night come rushing back to me.

I look wildly to the chair, searching for the knife I'd brought upstairs with me. It's nowhere to be found.

I'm immediately on edge when I return to my room, my hands trembling as I close the door behind me and try to catch my breath.

And in the glare of the sun, something shines from the center of my bed.

The knife.

5

LAYLA

"HAVE you ever lost your mind entirely before, Curtis?"

Curtis, who is currently fighting to get a chainsaw back in working order, looks up at me with a pinched expression. "I don't believe so, Miss Layla. But you look like you're fixin' to lose yours, I reckon."

Well, he's not wrong. I run my hand over my face, then through my hair, peering at the old handyman from my perch on the back porch. The overcast day is a welcome relief from the heat, and the choked tree line in the distance looks remarkably innocent compared to last night during the storm.

"You need sleep," he says in a fatherly tone that forces my gaze back to his face. "You look like you've been dragged to hell, and even hell didn't want ya and sent you packin'."

"That's the nicest thing anyone has ever said to me," I tease, rolling my eyes. "You're a real southern gentleman, Curtis."

He waves me off with one of his huge, calloused hands. Curtis is average height and portly, but his strength is truly incredible. His stained white shirt is coated in sweat while he yanks and fumbles with the chainsaw, mumbling curses under his breath.

I find his company comforting in a way I can't explain.

"Are there… big animals out here?"

"What do you mean?"

"Like…" I lean forward, resting my elbows on my knees as I look past him toward the trees in the distance. "Like, something big enough to make a lot of noise."

"Well, yes," he sighs, giving up on the chainsaw for the moment. "Why are you asking me this, Miss Layla?"

I roll my lower lip between my teeth and internally debate my options. Last night fucking sucked, plain and simple. I'm having a hard time deciding what was real, and what I made up in my fear fueled mind, in all honesty. The dream I had is one thing, but thinking I saw someone standing in the tree line still has me on edge.

Bailey hadn't arrived until almost 10:00 in the morning because of a downed tree in the road. I'd stayed up, going through almost every room in the entire house, all the way up to the fourth floor, where a decaying ladder dropped from the darkened entrance to the attic. I hadn't gone up there, of course. Who would? Most of the doors in the upper levels of the house were locked tight. I hadn't been sure what I'd been looking for, but I didn't find anything at all to ease my anxiety about the events of the night.

I'd even walked out here, to the backyard, and scoured the tree line for hours looking for something, anything, to prove that I'd actually seen someone standing out here in the rain.

I hadn't even found footprints. If there was evidence to be found, it had been washed away by the rain.

But the knife on my bed…

"We have raccoons out here that are a real problem," Curtis says with marked disdain. "They get into the house from time to time and cause a racket. Had some in the attic a year past. The smell–"

"What do they smell like?" I ask stupidly, my mind immediately lurching toward the memory of the musky, leathery scent I'd encountered during my nights alone in the house.

"Like trash, Miss Layla."

"Oh," I whisper to myself, closing my eyes for a moment.

When I open them again, Curtis is staring at me.

"You think I'm crazy." I give him a soft smile. "Don't you?"

"I think you're tired and letting this old house get to you." He walks up to the porch and leans on the railing, looking me in the eyes. "The old night nurse didn't sleep for weeks on end. Even during the day, she stayed up, wandering around and talking about hearing noises."

"What kind of noises?"

"Just old house noises, Miss Layla. The same noises you hear."

"What made her quit?"

"She never really quit; she just stopped coming. She was a young woman like yourself and stayed in the house like you, but one day she was just gone. She left everything behind and sped off in her car like she was being chased by something."

"That's awful!"

"Well, I'm just being honest with ya. You're a nurse, Miss Layla. You know the importance of sleep and what the lack of it can do to someone's mind." He let out a sigh, furrowing his brows at me. "You should get off the property from time to time, too. You haven't left since you got here two weeks ago."

"There's not much I need to be doing–"

"Well, you should find something, anything. Hell, come to church with Bailey on Sundays, our congregation would love to have ya."

"I'm not a church goin' girl," I say, mimicking his thick accent.

He frowns at me playfully. "Ah, well, neither was my wife, but now she teaches Sunday School. There's plenty of young men looking for a wife there too. It might be nice to have someone taking you on dates during the weekends."

A sharp clattering sound comes from high above our heads. Curtis glances up, squinting into the sun now peeking through the fast-moving clouds still heavy with rain.

Prickles of adrenaline ripple through my fingertips as I look up at the ceiling of the covered porch. "What was that?"

"Bailey must've dropped something is all."

"Do you really believe that?"

"I do," he says, meeting my eyes with a firm look that takes me slightly aback. "I believe there's nothin' sinister about this place. In fact–" he leans forward, crossing his arms, "I believe the only ghosts that inhabit old places like this are there because of ungodly people who've done unspeakable things."

"Doesn't this place have somewhat of a… sordid history?"

He frowns, narrowing his eyes at me. "You should be sleeping."

"Tell me what you know about this place. Please?" I bat my eyelashes at him.

He purses his lips, cocking his head to the side.

"You've been working here for decades from what Bailey said, surely you know something."

"I know a few things."

"Why won't you tell me?"

"None of it is rooted in fact, miss. I don't like spreading lies."

"Please!" I say again, with more force this time.

If Curtis can see the desperation behind my eyes, he doesn't show it. He just sighs, shifting his weight from foot to foot. "I don't believe in ghosts, I want that to be clear, you understand?"

"I understand."

He nods but looks conflicted. "This place used to be a plantation, you know. A real travesty, but those were the times unfortunately. The Gregorys were the first in this area to free their slaves, and that was years before the Civil War. They were hated for it, and it got violent." He sighs, shaking his head. "This house was actually built after the first house burned down… arson, of course. A few family members died in that fire, which is all public record."

Public record piques my interest.

He notices, adding. "All of this is available at the local library."

I nod, giving him a look that begs for him to go on. Another heavy sigh, and then he continues, "What's not in the public records is... a rumor that started somewhere around the turn of the century. A woman named Georgina Gregory, the young wife of Randolph Gregory, who owned the place in the early 1900s, was said to have been a witch with certain... tastes." He grimaces. "Randolph Gregory was a very old man, having been born in the original house and the one who built this one." He waves at the house. "He died under what is rumored to be suspicious circumstances, killed by a possible lover of the young Mrs. Gregory."

"Oh," I say, totally enraptured by what's becoming some incredibly juicy family drama. "Then what happened?"

"Well, their eldest son, Edward, became the man of the house. He went off to fight in World War I while his mother and two younger brothers remained here. However, when he was off at war, Georgina and the two younger boys perished in a fire in one of the outbuildings."

My stomach curls as he continues. "Edward Gregory came back to the states but didn't marry until the 1930s, and his wife gave him six children."

"Edward Gregory sounds familiar," I whisper, trying to link my family lines back to him. He must be my great-great-great-grandfather, or something.

"His son Andrew became the heir after his untimely, rather young, death. The rest of the Gregory children spread out. There were three girls born in the '40s, and two other boys, beside Andrew. Herbert and Roger."

"Roger is my grandfather," I tell him, and he nods, like he knows this. "So... Andrew is Aunt Penny's father?"

"Yes ma'am."

I resist the urge to wring my hands in anticipation for whatever he's going to say next, but he gets a distant look in his eyes. "Ms. Penny was his only child for a long time. He and his wife desperately wanted more, and... well, the story goes, Andrew Gregory sought the help of.... Well, it's a rumor."

"Tell me!"

"Witches from around these parts…. I don't believe in them, just so we're clear, but the troubling thing is that Mr. Gregory started acting real strange, more aggressive, more reclusive, shut himself and his family up in this house for years. Mrs. Gregory was a frail little thing, much like Ms. Penny is now, and shouldn't have been trying to have any more babies. Ms. Penny got sent to a Catholic boarding school in New Orleans and was away from most of what happened, I believe. I was just a kid then, you know. Lapping up these rumors like a cat with cream."

"You probably heard a rendition of the rumors I've heard from my own family," I interrupt, starting to lose patience as the hair on the back of my neck starts to stand on end. Again, I feel like I'm being watched, like someone is standing behind me.

"Then you'll know Mrs. Gregory went insane and died in an asylum."

"Yes–"

"Andrew Gregory, according to the rumor mill, went to a witch doctor, took poor Mrs. Gregory with him. I don't know what they did to that poor woman, but she was never the same. They did have a son, but he died shortly after he was born. That baby was born too early, and real sick, and in those times there wasn't much that could be done for an early baby like that. All the stories I was told, however, were real awful, miss. I have a hard time even saying it out loud, but…." He sucks in a breath, fixing me with a look that makes the gooseflesh ripple over my arms. "They say Mr. Gregory wasn't the child's father, that the father was some kind of demon, and Mrs. Gregory begged him to kill the baby, to take it out to the swamp and drown him. I don't know if that's actually what happened, but there was no funeral for that child. No christening neither. Nobody saw him, not even Ms. Penny."

I find it hard to swallow.

He continues. "Afterward, Mr. Gregory was found dead in the cigar room upstairs, and Mrs. Gregory had her psychotic break. Poor Ms. Penny was only sixteen when her mother died, and she left school to come here. She's been alone ever since. Never married, never went back into town."

"And you said this house isn't haunted," I choke out. "How many people have died here?"

"Who can say? This is an old place, Miss Layla. But, I'll tell ya, I've been working here for forty years now, and I ain't never once seen a ghost. Never felt like there was one around, neither. And I'll tell ya, I've been to some real haunted places in my time, especially up in New Orleans. Now there's a place with ghosts, I'll say."

"Well–"

"Well, nothing," he says, giving me another fatherly look of disapproval. "I told you what I know, and now it's time for you to get to bed, young lady."

I pout but obey him nonetheless. He goes back to trying to fix his chainsaw while I seemingly float through the house, so tired I barely register my movements until I find myself in my room, staring down at my bed.

How am I supposed to sleep now, knowing what I know about this family? My family, in fact.

Somehow, I manage. I fall face first into bed and wake up four hours later. The sun is still high in the sky, but the clock on the wall reads 4:44. My alarm goes off like clockwork at 4:45, and I roll out of bed to start another shift alone in this creepy house.

By the time I walk downstairs, Bailey is hiking her purse over her shoulder in the front foyer. "Oh, there you are! I didn't want to wake you up, but...." She steps forward as I reach the foyer. "Look, my cousin is taking me to New Orleans two weeks from now for a weekend trip in the big city. I'd like you to come, Layla. I think you need to get out of the house for a bit. Vera's got everything covered for us on the weekend anyway."

"Sure," I tell her, still half asleep.

Bailey beams. "Great. It's a plan, then. I made some fresh coffee if you want some. It's piping hot."

"Thanks, Bailey."

She gives me her typical kind smile and leaves. I watch her rusted car bounce out of the driveway before turning to the kitchen, following the scent of freshly brewed coffee.

But when I enter the kitchen, I'm not alone.

I scream, absolutely startled, as the stranger turns around, his green eyes meeting mine.

6

DALTON

I CATCH the screaming night nurse by the wrist before she can flee back into the hallway. Her deep blue eyes shine like smooth sapphires, alight with fear. "Someone's on edge," I say, letting go of her wrist, hoping my touch is enough to tell her I'm real and not one of the many apparitions who haunt this hellhole.

I can almost taste her fear. She gapes at me, looking me up and down. "Who the *hell* are you?"

"Who are you?" I ask, sipping from the coffee Bailey so generously made before taking her leave this evening.

"Who am I?" she says, stupidly–if I might add.

"Uh, yeah?" I stare down at her, drinking her in. Bouncy, thick blonde hair that would probably touch her lower back if she didn't keep it piled on the top of her head. Slim shoulders, narrow waist. A great rack I'd like to paint if I could ever get her naked. Her nipples are peaked under her white tank-top, and she isn't wearing a bra, of course. These night nurses get comfortable, fast, especially when they think they're alone in this big house.

Her Barbie face twists into a scowl as I slowly rake my gaze from her chest back to her eyes, which are furious.

"I'm Dalton. Nice to meet you... well, you haven't told me your name."

"Who are you and what are you doing here?"

"I live here."

"No–"

I step toward her, and she steps back, her body colliding with the wall next to the doorway I'm sure she was aiming for. She looks down at my shirt, which is splattered with paint, and then my wrists and hands, which are also covered in paint. Suddenly, her demeanor shifts, and her eyes soften, her mouth ticking up in a beautiful smile.

I liked her better when she looked scared.

"Oh, you must be the *painter*!" She laughs, running her hand over her face. "God, you scared me to death. Mr. Wilson came over the other day and was talking about how someone had been restoring the old wallpaper in the dining room."

"Hmm." I match her smile. "That would be me."

"I didn't realize you lived here, though?"

"I'm a boarder, you could say. Ms. Gregory allows me a studio and bedroom while I'm working here and in the area."

"I haven't seen you around," she says, her voice soft and sweet. I bet her lips taste like honey–and her cunt. I'll be the judge of that eventually, I'm sure.

"I've been in New Orleans for a job. I just got back," I tell her.

"Then you'll be here for a while?"

"That depends on how quickly I can get my work done. I'd like to move on from this place, eventually."

"You don't like it here?"

I'm still standing close enough to be in her personal space, but she hasn't moved, so I haven't either. I'm inches away from being able to cage her against that wall behind her. I'm in a rush, however, and bring my coffee to my lips, smiling over the rim. "It's a creepy old house. I don't sleep well when I'm here."

She melts into my hands, just like that.

I take a step back and turn to the counter, waiting for her to take the bait. She will, I'm sure.

She steps up beside me and pours herself a cup of coffee. "It is kind of a creepy place, isn't it?"

"I don't like the banging in the night," I agree.

"Do you ever feel like you're being… watched?"

"Oh, all the time." I smile down at her again, noticing the way her shoulders slump with relief. "It's haunted, you know."

"I don't think so…. You know Curtis, I'm guessing? He told me it's not."

"Curtis doesn't know shit."

She frowns at me, leaning her hip against the counter. "Why would I believe a perfect stranger over him?"

"Well, I'm not a perfect stranger anymore, am I? You're technically the stranger. You haven't even told me your name."

She blushes as I fix her with an intense stare. Her eyes meet mine, and she shrugs. "It's Layla."

"Layla," I repeat, drawing it out like I'm brushing it over her skin. "That's not a bad name at all."

"Well, thanks," she grumbles, straightening up to fetch the creamer out of the fridge. "So, you're going to be here for a while then?"

"I already said so–"

"When did you get here, exactly?"

"Oh, early this morning. I don't exactly remember."

She freezes, her hand resting on the fridge door. "During the storm?"

"Yeah, so?"

"What time, exactly?"

"I couldn't say."

She narrows her eyes at me then drops her gaze to my plain gray shirt and jeans. She lingers for a while on my hair, which is a little longer than I'd like it to be right now, then drops her gaze to my unshaven jaw.

"What, Layla?"

"Were you out back around five in the morning?"

"In the rain? Why would I do that?"

She holds my gaze for a few seconds. "No reason–"

"Are you seeing things you can't explain?"

She pours creamer in her coffee and refuses to meet my eyes, but her cheeks flush.

"Maybe having… dreams–"

Her eyes snap to mine, her cheeks now burning a fiery crimson. "How did you…. No, I'm not," she snaps. "You're just trying to scare me."

"I don't even know you. Why would I be trying to scare you?"

She keeps her eyes on mine as she takes a sip of her drink. She looks me up and down like she's deciding whether I'm a threat or not. "I'm sorry I scared you earlier. I figured someone told you I'd be here eventually," I continue.

"No one told me anything," she says with a marked attitude. "How do I know you're not lying, and you're actually about to murder me and loot the house?"

"There's nothing here that I want," I laugh. "And… I certainly wouldn't waste that kind of time on you, Angel."

Something flashes behind her eyes, but she steels her expression and turns from me, heading toward the hallway.

"Watch out for yourself," I tell her in passing, but she turns her head.

"What do you mean?"

"This old house has a way of getting into people's heads. You should know that already, I'm sure, given what happened to the last night nurse."

She turns just enough that I can see her entire face. "What happened to her? I was told she just left."

"Oh, she left. *Screaming.*" I raise the coffee to my lips.

"You're just trying to scare me."

"I'm being honest with you. If you can feel something in this house, see things that shouldn't be there… you should be on your guard, Layla. And, while I'm at it, stay out of my way. I'll be busy on the third floor, and I don't like being interrupted."

"You're a real prick, you know that?"

"I'm honest," I tell her. "And I'm telling you to reexamine what you think you see in darkened corners and lurking in the tree line."

Another flush drifts over her face. She turns abruptly and walks away, out of sight.

But she's not out of mind as I make my way upstairs to my studio on the third floor. I set my coffee down and pull dust laden sheets from the easels and workbenches, cursing under my breath at the state things have been left in. I pull out some paper and sit down at my desk, beginning a sketch. Layla's face comes takes form on the page with each stroke.

"This one is mine," I say in a whisper to the room around me, to each darkened corner. "She's off limits. She's *mine*."

7

LAYLA

I HAVE A TYPE, I'll admit. Tall, dark, handsome, and mysterious. Dalton, unfortunately, checks off all of those boxes, even if our introductory conversation took an abrupt turn.

He obviously picked up on my irrational fear of the house somehow and decided to spin it to his advantage. I got the sense, during our short time together in the kitchen, that he enjoyed trying to scare me.

After my conversation with Curtis, I'd come to the conclusion that the house might just harbor bad memories but not ghosts and ghouls. I'd never outwardly admit that I'm more in tune with the energy of certain places, but after working in hospitals my entire career, I've often wondered if the things I've seen and heard held weight and weren't just tricks of my mind.

Still, having someone else in the house now makes me feel slightly more secure in my surroundings as I go through my nightly routine with Aunt Penny.

She's not nearly as lively tonight as she was during the storm last night. Her eyelids are heavy as I sit in the chair and read another three chapters of the novel we started a few days ago. Her slow, rhythmic heartbeat sends soft beeps through the room as I feel my eyes starting to sag, the room around me going dark around the edges. I only got a few hours of sleep today, and it's not enough.

I set the book down and rub my eyes before glancing over at my aunt. It's 3:00 in the morning, and she's asleep, her face relaxed and peaceful and her hands folded over her lap.

"I'll come check on you in a little while," I tell her and turn off the remaining light in the room before crossing the hallway into my own room, shutting the door behind me and locking it.

Darkness sweeps over the space, nothing but moonlight illuminating my unmade bed. The floorboards creak as I walk to the bed and slide into the moon drenched covers, pulling them up to my chin.

But I lie awake with my eyes wide open, afraid to close them.

Dalton mentioned dreams earlier. He also called me *Angel*, just like the stranger in my dream had whispered while he fucked me. My body tightens at the memory. Unlike my usual, fractured dreams, these felt so real, and I remembered every moment after I woke up.

I need to sleep. I need a few solid hours of rest, or I could very well lose my mind, just like Curtis said. I'm afraid I'm already halfway there when the creaking of the pipes begins, mingling with my ragged breath. I pull the covers higher, as if they can shield me from every bump and scratch in the night.

Is Dalton awake upstairs, painting?

Does he hear that strange, rhythmic scratching sound too?

I close my eyes, and my body relaxes into sleep, my mind drifting in darkness for a long time.

"I keep telling you to stay out of this," Dalton says, his voice far away and distorted. I turn to him, and the dining room comes into view, the wallpaper glistening and trembling like it's come alive. "I warned you, Layla, what would happen—"

"I don't care," I tell him, walking toward him, running my fingertips over his broad, chiseled chest.

"You love these games, don't you, Angel?" he whispers into my ear, his dark brown hair tickling my cheek. "Fear turns you on, doesn't it?"

I let out my breath in a whimper as his hands clutch my waist, his fingers digging into my skin.

"You love being hunted, don't you?"

I practically purr with anticipation when his hands graze over my ass and thighs.

"Do you want me to hunt you down and have my way with you, Angel?"

Suddenly, I'm outside of the house. It's dark and raining so hard I can feel the icy, unforgiving droplets slicing into my skin. I'm running, sprinting for my life, but my body won't move fast enough. It's like I'm moving in slow motion, and whatever's behind me is gaining on me. I trip, falling an impossible distance down to the ground through total darkness.

"I warned you this wouldn't end well for us. I tried to help you. I tried to save you."

I wake with a start, my body coated in sweat and a throbbing ache between my thighs. I sit up, rubbing sleep from my eyes as the room around me comes into view. It's still dark, the moonlight now fractured by heavy clouds. Rain drizzles down the warped windows as I slide my legs out of bed and stretch my arms over my head. I'd set my alarm for 6:00 A.M., but it's only 5:00, which means I slept for at least three hours.

That's good enough for now. Good enough to feel slightly refreshed, anyway.

"Why keep playing?"

I freeze, blinking into the darkness.

"Amos—"

The tablet on my dresser lights up, a soft alarm going off to alert me of movement in my aunt's room. I pad across the floorboards, careful not to make any noise, and snatch the tablet off the dresser. I pull up the video feed, then her vitals, which are normal. The room is empty, dark, and silent. Am I still dreaming?

"What do you gain from this?" Aunt Penny asks, her words clear and sharp. A chill licks up my spine as I watch the video feed, unable to blink.

Who is she talking to?

"Go away. Leave me be." Her lips barely move, and her eyes are closed.

Silence settles, but I sit on the edge of my bed looking down at the tablet for another twenty minutes before I finally set it down and rest my face in my hands. She'd just been dreaming, that's all. I rarely hear her speak, so it's strange when she does. That's it.

Footsteps in the hallway break me out of my downward spiral. They come to a halt in front of my door, and I jump when a sharp knock echoes through my room. "H-Hello?"

The door swings open, and Dalton steps inside my room, his body taking up the threshold as he looks around, a cup of coffee in his hand. He lifts it to his lips as he peers around the room–at the suitcase I've yet to fully unpack and my messy vanity, then my unmade bed.

I swear I locked the door.

"Can I help you?" I ask, swallowing against the tightness in my throat as I glance at the tablet sitting beside me on the bed.

"I was just making sure you're awake." His eyes–the color of polished jade–meet mine, then slowly rake over my face. Dalton is exceedingly handsome, and he knows it. He oozes the kind of charm men who know they're good looking have down to a fine science.

"I don't need you to wake me up in the morning. I have an alarm set on my phone."

He shrugs, leaning on the doorframe. "Sleep well?"

I narrow my eyes at him. He's wearing an old black shirt and gray joggers that hug his muscled frame, his dark softly curled hair ruffled from sleep. Unshaven with his eyes slightly puffy, I gather he likely just woke up as well and that he didn't sleep much either.

His mouth ticks up at the corners as he continues to stare at me. "What's with the look?"

"What look?"

"You're scowling at me."

"You're in my room right now, uninvited."

With an arch of a dark brow, he drawls, "Are you saying you'd invite me to your room sometime, Angel?"

"First of all," I snap, rising from the bed with my hands firmly planted on my hips, "my name is Layla, not *Angel*. In fact, you can call me Miss Bryant or Nurse Bryant." Dalton is nothing but amused as I continue, "Secondly, get out of my room!"

"Lock the door next time." He gives me a devilish smile and turns toward the hallway.

"I did lock the door." My voice cracks, giving way to that creeping, anxious fear I've been trying to keep tamped down since I came to this place.

He looks at me over his shoulder, his expression shifting from saccharine charm to something darker, more knowing. "I think you'll find that that doesn't usually make a difference here." With that, he simply walks away, leaving my door wide open.

I have it in mind to chase him down and ask what the hell he meant by that, but a soft alarm begins to ring through the room. It's already 6:00 now. How had an hour passed so quickly without me realizing it?

"Shit," I whisper, turning off the alarm and darting between the bathroom and my dresser as I pull on a pair of creamy taupe colored scrubs and pull my hair into a bun. The humidity makes my usually lackluster waves coil into curls around my shoulders, with a fluffy layer of frizz rising like a halo around my face. I ignore my reflection and stoop, pulling on my sneakers before leaving the room and hurrying downstairs to start the last few hours of my shift.

But to my surprise, Vera, the weekend nurse, is already in the supply room filling a tray with my aunt's morning medications.

"V-Vera!" I gasp, startled by her presence.

Vera turns around, looks me up and down, and turns back to her work. "Did you forget what day it was?"

I blink, watching the older woman flutter around the room for a moment. Metal shelves reach to the plastered ceiling, everything washed in gray early morning sunlight, highlighting the silver streaks in Vera's pin-straight hair that dusts over her narrow, impossibly slim shoulders. Vera can't be more than one hundred pounds. I'm on the short side at five foot three, but Vera looks to be much shorter than me.

She hustles past me while I try to get my bearings. "It's–it's Saturday?"

"Yes." Vera nods, rolling her eyes. "Very good. What happens on Saturday?"

I don't like her patronizing tone, but this is just Vera. She doesn't like anyone, especially me. "It's your shift but–but you've never been here this early–"

"Miss Bailey is picking you up to go to New Orleans this weekend, remember?"

"Oh, shit, I forgot." I run my hand over my face, peeking at her through my fingers. "Wait, no, she said the trip was in like, two weeks?"

Vera gives me an exasperated look and motions her hand toward a calendar hanging on the wall beside her head. "Are you losing your mind, Miss Bryant?"

I might be. I step forward, my eyes locked on the calendar. How is it almost July already? Had weeks seriously passed without me realizing it? I swear the last time I spoke to Bailey had been yesterday after her shift, and she asked me to go on this trip with her... two weeks from *now*.

I blow out my breath and look down at Vera, who is examining my expression carefully. "I didn't get much sleep the last few days, I think. I must have forgotten about this entirely."

Vera's dark eyes search mine before she says, "She won't be here until eleven. Go back to sleep after filling me in on your shift."

I nod, my fingertips prickling as unease drifts over my skin, making me shiver. "It was a quiet night. Her vitals were fine, everything in the green. She did... she did talk to herself this morning, loud enough it activated the cameras in her room." I hand Vera the tablet.

"She must be feeling well, then. She rarely talks anymore. That new blood pressure medication must be working as intended."

"It's making it hard for her to sleep, though–"

"Her doctor is making a trip to Hahnville next week. I'm sure Bailey will bring it up to him." Vera walks away without another word, leaving me utterly alone in the supply room.

I scratch my head as I look back at the calendar, unsure of what to think, what to do.

"Coffee," I breathe. That's what I need right now.

The kitchen isn't empty when I walk into the room with the startlingly green vinyl floor. Dalton stands by the sink, washing several paintbrushes as he looks out the back window with a blank expression. Blood red paint swirls down the drain. I ignore his presence and pour myself some coffee and walk right out the back door, sitting down on the steps.

I watch the sunrise over the cypress grove and cemetery in the distance, light pink and gold rays of morning sun falling in ribbons over the marsh that hugs the house.

Something is wrong with this place, I decide. And whatever it is, it's sunk its claws into me.

I can't let that continue to happen.

8

DALTON

THE CIGAR ROOM on the second floor has been untouched since the early 1930s. The moth-eaten fabric that covers the furniture smells sharply of damp and mildew, and the once lively floral wallpaper is peeling from the walls, revealing horse-hair plaster beneath.

I huff a breath as I look around, the darkened corners of the wide, square room beckoning to me. I ignore it, like usual, but that creeping sensation licking up my neck continually steals my attention as I lay out sheets of plastic across the mahogany floor and prepare to repair what wallpaper I can salvage.

I'm not sure how I got into this line of work. My dad had been a contractor, and since it had just been me and him growing up, I spent a great deal of time following him from job site to job site, mingling with the various tradesmen and technicians he worked with day in and day out. He got a job in the Garden District in New Orleans—fixing up an old Greek Revival mansion. That's where I'd met the teams who spend hours upon hours meticulously restoring historic homes to their former glory, despite the cost and time spent. Most people would have suggested tearing this room down to the studs and starting over.

Hell, most people would have razed this house, drained the marsh, and built something new.

But that's the thing about these old Louisiana families with their old money and vile pasts that gave them their fortunes in the first place. They want everything to stay just like it was, just like it's always been. Change is their constant enemy.

I crouch, mixing a sheer plaster base coat in a five gallon bucket. I've already cleaned and sprayed the room, trying to cut down on the dust and mold likely spawning behind the wallpaper. The Gregorys don't care about that. None of these old families do. They want their houses to shine like a beckon to an era when they were kings and queens, and their entire day was spent counting their coins and drinking champagne.

Ms. Gregory wants the house fixed up. It had been the last request she'd made before her condition escalated. That was ten years ago now, and I'm the fifth painter who has graced this house with my skill set.

I'm only here because I've lasted longer than the rest.

The house wants to rot, to succumb to the marsh and the shadows of the cypress grove.

I stand and look out the window at the wide, cracked driveway as an unfamiliar car rolls to a stop. I narrow my eyes at the man who steps out, a hand raised to shield his face from the sun.

Bailey, the day nurse, gets out of the passenger side and waves toward the porch where Layla has just stepped outside dressed for a journey.

Her white sundress shows off her muscled legs, her skin kissed by the sun. Her golden blonde hair is braided down her back as she walks over to Bailey and excitedly converses with her before they disappear into the car with the man. I watch Layla climb into the back seat, her white teeth gleaming in the sunlight as she pulls the door closed.

She thinks leaving this place will give her the clarity she's desperate for. She's wrong. She should never have come here. Ms. Gregory spent decades keeping her family–especially the young, impressionable women–away from this house.

That idiot lawyer in Hahnville fucked it all up, and Ms. Gregory is too far gone to do anything about it now.

I roll my lower lip between my teeth as I watch the car speed down the driveway, the vines hanging from the trees scraping across the sunroof while dust kicks up in its wake.

Layla could drive hundreds of miles away from this place, and it wouldn't matter. She's already trapped, just like me. Just like everyone who came before us, and those that will come after.

Hours pass. I press the remains of the wallpaper back to the plaster, securing it in place. I sketch the wallpaper in the areas where it's withered and melted away, preparing to patch it with hand-painted wallpaper that, in the end, will match the original so perfectly no one who comes into this derelict room will know the difference.

The sun is setting by the time I leave the cigar room and walk upstairs. My studio is bathed in golden light that shreds the lingering shadows and sends warmth throughout the room.

"I asked you to stop moving things around," I grumble to myself, sitting down on a stool and edging closer to the canvas resting on an easel by the window. I give it a single glance, frowning at the shocking dark red paint seeping through the hand-stretched canvas. I shove the canvas off the easel, letting it fall to the ground. "Fuck off, seriously."

I'm answered by silence.

I spend the rest of the day practicing the gentle strokes needed to mimic the petals and stems on the wallpaper downstairs. Night falls before I finally leave my stool and go stand by the window. I pull a cigarette out of my pocket and light it, taking a long drag as I watch the trees dance in a light breeze. No storms tonight, at least not for the next few hours.

A figure moves between the trees, taunting me. I arch my brows as it skirts across the tree line across from the driveway and disappears into the shadows.

This fucking house.

I turn back to my easel and find the canvas I'd discarded earlier is back in place. A half-finished portrait of Layla stares back at me.

I take another drag from my cigarette and lean against the windowsill, staring into those big blue eyes. Blood red paint drips from her lashes and nose, rolling down to the bottom of the canvas.

I should leave her alone. There's no reason for me to have taunted her like I did the other day, but something about her presence here unnerves me. She's not supposed to be here. She can't be here. But that doesn't mean I can't have a little fun while I do what I can to send her running back to wherever the hell she came from in hopes she's still got a fucking chance of walking away from this unscathed.

She's in New Orleans tonight. Maybe that's a good thing, given how active the dark corners in the house are tonight. A scratching sound—like nails along a chalkboard—scurries overhead, knocking dust loose from the rafters.

The house doesn't like that she left.

I smirk at the thought, then take the painting off the easel while pinching my cigarette between my lips. I send my knee through it and let it drop to the ground.

"Leave her the fuck alone." I pick up my car keys from the table next to the door and leave, unsure of where I'm going, but I can't stay here.

9

LAYLA

THE BLACK PENNY in the French Quarter is definitely a dive, but everything is all lush, dark paint and leather, as I follow Bailey and her cousin, Adam, through the darkened threshold into the bar. Beyond the bar, the sidewalk is teeming with nightlife. Music flows through the street, mingling with riotous chatter and the occasionally drunken body swaying to the music in the middle of the road.

We'd spent the day exploring New Orleans. I'm full of beignets, and my ears are ringing from the sweet sound of a saxophone as we saddle up to a high-top table near the front of the bar. Adam leaves to order drinks, disappearing into the throng of jazz music and lively conversation.

"I'm so glad you came with us tonight!" Bailey exclaims over the noise, leaning in to brush the words directly into my ear. "You've been in a trance the past couple of weeks. I thought I'd never be able to get you out of the house!"

"What do you mean?" Leaving Hahnville is a nice distraction from the fact that two weeks had flashed before my eyes without me realizing it. I'd come to the conclusion I'm just severely sleep deprived. There were times during my travel nursing rotations that I looked at a calendar and realized weeks had gone by in a blink, having been too busy to notice the passage of time. But I'd been an ER nurse then–burnt out, worn thin, living off energy drinks and stale granola bars. Working for my aunt has been a much slower pace of life. I shouldn't be this burnt out, not yet at least.

"Curtis told me you haven't slept more than two to three hours a day since you came to the house," she scolds. "And he's right. You've just been wandering around all day until your shift at night!"

"I have trouble sleeping in the house!" I have to yell over the music.

I'm not sure if Bailey hears me or not. "You should order some black out curtains for your room. That should help!"

"What?!" Our cheeks are practically touching as we yell back and forth. A new band has entered the stage, and fresh music is fanning out over the crowd, which is going absolutely feral. "What did you say?"

Adam slides up to us, handing me a gin cocktail. He is ridiculously good looking, but I'm not his type. In fact, his boyfriend, Carlos, is currently trying to fight his way to our high-top table through the maddening fray of partiers trying to shove toward the stage.

"This place is insane tonight, Adam! Let's go to Old River Blues instead!" Carlos manages to say as he hugs the table, panting.

"They're closed until next weekend!" Adam shouts over the rim of his neat glass of whiskey, his smooth brown skin illuminated by the dimly flashing lights all around us. "I don't know why. That was the original plan–"

Their voices are drowned out by the music. I stand on my tiptoes to look out over the crowd. The music isn't what I expected. After a day full of jazz, this new band's music blends into something more sensational, a mix between jazz and EDM. They are playing an ethereal, sultry song that sends shivers shooting up my spine and settling deep in my bones, begging me to dance, to sway my hips to the music.

I sip my drink, turning back to Bailey, who is watching the crowd with interest. I follow her gaze to a group of men standing on the outskirts of the crowded dance floor. A man with dark hair and gray eyes bright enough to be seen through the crowd looks right at Bailey and lifts his drink in greeting, his mouth quirking into a seductive smirk.

"You should go talk to him!" I shout, nudging her with my shoulder.

"I'll go if you come with me. It looks like he has plenty of friends to choose from!"

She throws me a devilish smile, winks, and the rest is history.

I'm allowed to have a little fun, aren't I?

"What's your name!?" the tall, fit, blond man with devastatingly dark eyes asks as he leans down, his cheek brushing against the top of my head.

"Layla!"

"Nice to meet you Layla." His eyes light on mine, the color of fine whiskey, in my humble opinion. "I'm Nick."

I've decided Nick will do nicely. I've already learned this group of guys are on vacation, having flown down from New York City to spend a weekend of debauchery in New Orleans. They're all finance bros, of course, and are more than willing to pepper both me and Bailey in attention and all of the drinks our pretty little heart's desire.

But I'm already two gin and sodas in, and my body is feeling loose and relaxed. I subconsciously sway to the music, which beckons me to join the crowded dance floor with each seductive note.

Nick and his buddies don't seem too keen on dancing tonight. I doubt any of them would risk getting sweat and glitter on their dry-clean-only Ralph Lauren button-down shirts.

"Where are you going, Layla?" he asks.

I reach up toward the ceiling, closing my eyes as my hips sway to the thrumming echo of the music. "Dancing! Come with me!" I open my eyes to see Nick watching me with a hungry look behind his gaze, but finance bro from New York City doesn't follow me into the crowd right away, and within seconds I'm consumed by the throng.

Each note is a siren song. Each chord buries itself in every cell of my body. I close my eyes and move to the music, letting my mind go blissfully blank. There're people all around me, everyone in their own little world. I feel like I've been cast under a spell, and there's nothing on this earth that could tear me from this feeling of utter bliss.

I love to dance. I love that high brought on by hot, sweaty clubs where the music is loud enough to drown out my inner voice. I love the feeling of strangers surrounding me, of being totally unknown and vulnerable, with no cares but the way the music settles in my heart and sets my blood on fire.

I don't open my eyes when I feel two large hands graze over my hips and stomach. I let my head fall back against the chest of someone at least a foot taller than me, relaxing into his touch as he presses my ass against his thighs and grinds against me to the music. Did Nick finally decide to follow me? The flashing lights blur my senses, and then there's nothing but the music and this strangers touch, and I'm lost to it, wholly and utterly overcome.

His fingertips travel up my belly, over the ruching of the tight, light blue dress I bought at a boutique earlier today. One of his hands rests over my navel while the other moves upward, over my breasts, his tender, exploratory touch sending ripples of heat washing over my skin. His hand slides up further and closes around my throat.

I jerk in shock, but his hand on my belly keeps me fixed in place, pressed against him as my eyes fly open.

"Are you afraid?"

I let out what breath I can muster, trying to see and hear past the shimmering lights and throbbing music, but everything is all shadow now. All of the colors and sounds merge together, and my vision begins to blur as his hand tightens around my neck.

"I could take you right here, and no one would even hear you scream."

His hand slips down from my belly and under my dress. I jerk involuntarily as his fingers brush over my panties. I'm ashamed of how wet I am right now, how turned on being this vulnerable makes me. His dominating touch has me melting into his hands–this total stranger–this man whose face I haven't turned to look at.

But his voice is so familiar. So very familiar….

I close my eyes as he slides a finger over my slit, my underwear the only barrier between us.

"You're so fucking wet," he rasps against my cheek, groaning with approval. His teeth graze the rim of my ear, his breath tickling my skin.

My eyelids flutter closed as he slides his fingers under my panties, pushing them to the side. He grinds against me, his groans mingling with the sultry, thrumming music that sends vibrations up through the floorboards. I writhe against his touch, unable to help it, and I know full well how wrong this is.

But I it turns me on. I've always craved this. For years, I've dreamed of being chased, being taken, being treated like a prize and used like a toy.

But I've never let it show. I've never had the nerve to ask anyone to be rough with me. To fuck me in public like this total stranger is trying to do. And God, I'll let him.

I reach back and grip his thighs, which are thick, solid muscle beneath my hands. He could rip me apart. This guy could pick me up and haul me over his shoulder with ease or throw me down and have his way with me right here. Fighting back would be futile.

But I don't want to fight back.

"Please," I pant, my head resting on his chest as he slowly, achingly, circles his thumb over my clit.

"You haven't earned it yet."

The room spins on its axis, and suddenly it's Dalton holding me. It's Dalton's hand clutching my throat and his fingers pumping inside of me in the middle of the dance floor. His teeth graze my neck as he laughs, low and maliciously, while my body suddenly erupts in chills that send tremors through every muscle and bone.

He's the only reason I'm upright. My legs shake as his touch deepens, becoming more aggressive, like he can feel I'm on the edge of release.

"You're mine," he growls. *"Don't forget that."*

My lips part as I fight back a moan, but then my name rips through the air. "LAYLA! Layla? Where the hell is she?"

His touch evaporates, and I whirl around, panting, finding myself alone in the crowd. Dalton, Nick, or whoever it had been–is gone.

My heart rate spikes, and I find it hard to breathe as I frantically look around. My head spins from the gin and dancing. Sweat breaks out along my temples. I made it up, didn't I? This is another dream. I'm losing my fucking mind… but then my blood runs cold anew as the music shifts, and the band begins to play a familiar song. It's a sped up, modern version, but those lyrics sink into my skin like claws. *"She's stretched on a long, white table. So sweet, so cold, so fair…"*

"St. James Infirmary," I whisper.

"Layla!" Bailey beams as she shoves into view, but her smile falters when she sees the troubled expression on my face. "Oh my God, what happened? Are you all right?"

"I don't feel well. I–I drank too much–" I resist the sudden urge to vomit as I push past her and the crowd, fighting my way toward the edge of the dance floor. The music is grating on my nerves, setting every fiber of my being on fire as I try to clear my vision. Adam and Carlos are still at the high-top, and Carlos stands when he sees me approaching.

"Are you okay?" he asks, but I shake my head, covering my mouth with my hands. Adam springs into action, and in a matter of seconds, I'm being hustled outside in the cool, late night air.

I steady myself on the side of the building, my heart refusing to stop hammering against my ribs. Adam is saying something to me, but the blood rushing through my ears blocks out his voice. With my phone in my hands, I tell them, "I just ordered a car." My words are strained and falling over each other. "I'm going back to Hahnville."

"If you wait, I'll get Bailey, and we can drive you back–"

I shake my head, waving him away. "I'm not going to ruin her weekend away. I'm fine, really. I'm just going to wait for the car. It's fine. I'm fine. *Everything's fine.*" My words are slurred from the gin, I think. Either the gin, or the adrenaline pumping through my veins. My vision is still blurred, but in a matter of seconds, an Uber pulls up along the busy sidewalk. Adam, ever the gentleman, steps forward and speaks with the driver for a moment before waving me over.

"Take her straight there, no stops." He slips the stranger a hundred dollar bill. "Call me when she gets there safely. This is my number–"

"You didn't have to do that," I try to say, but my throat closes around the words as I slouch into the backseat and close my eyes.

New Orleans spins out of view while I rest my head on the door, refusing to close my eyes and let the darkness still hovering within my peripheral vision take over. It's only a thirty minute drive, and a silent one, nothing but soft music on the radio to drown out the blood still thrumming in my ears.

I'm insane for thinking Dalton had been at that club. What are the odds? But if it had been him....

10

Layla

"Uh, is this the address?"

I look up, blinking to clear my blurry vision, and see that we're idling at the rusted front gate to the Gregory Estate.

"Yeah, this is it."

"I gotta be honest with you, ma'am. I don't think my car is going to get down the driveway." My driver's not wrong. His sedan practically scrapes the ground as he pulls forward. The decaying concrete juts up in places, forced skyward by the relentless roots cutting through the cement.

"It's fine. I can walk."

"You sure? I could walk you down–"

"Don't worry about it," I mumble, letting myself out of the car and shutting the door behind me. I take off my heels and rest my bare feet on the cool, solid ground. It feels good. The air is heavy with humidity, but a slight, chilled breeze clears my head enough for my gin-induced stupor to finally give way. "Thanks for the ride."

With that, I walk away, the Uber's headlights fading behind me. Eventually, I hear the driver carefully turn his car around and speed off into the night, leaving me alone with nothing but swampy darkness as company.

Cicadas hum and chirp all around me as I pad barefoot down the long, winding driveway. The long walk cuts through my buzz like a blade, knocking me down a few pegs. I blink up at the clear night sky and take a deep, restorative breath. I hadn't had a sip of alcohol since I started working here, and I went straight to gin, my arch nemesis? No wonder I practically hallucinated on the dance floor. I'm not even sure anyone had been dancing with me now that I have a clearer picture of the situation. Just like my weird, illicit dreams, this is obviously something I cooked up in my absolutely deranged and sex-starved mind.

Right?

"I need to get laid," I grumble to myself, swinging my strappy heels as the house comes into view.

A snapping sound catches my attention, and I whirl around.

Someone is standing fifty yards away in the shadow of the trees, and this time, I'm sure what I'm seeing is *real*.

Whether from the lingering whispers of liquid courage in my veins, or an onslaught of fresh adrenaline, I puff up my shoulders and glower at the shadows, my eyes locked on the figure now walking in my direction. "Hey!" I shout, and not kindly. "What are you doing out here in the dark? Go away!"

The figure stops walking and stands just out of sight, nothing but the outline of their body visible to my eyes, which are strained from having to peer through the darkness.

A shimmering red light erupts–the cherry of a cigarette–and for whatever reason, that calms me down significantly. This is real. This is happening. There's actually someone standing mere yards away in the darkness, and it's not a trick of my mind this time.

"What the *fuck* are you doing out here barefoot, Layla?"

I sag with relief. "I could ask you why you're here, too."

Dalton comes into view. In the near total darkness, his features are shadowed, nothing but the brief outline of his lit cigarette to cast a shred of light over his chiseled face. Compared to the finance bros from the club, Dalton is ruggedly handsome with an edge of mystery I find fascinating, not the classically charming Ivy League type at all. He's the type of guy I'd expect to run into at a dark poetry reading at a bookstore in Seattle, and that's not a bad thing.

"I didn't know you smoked."

He shrugs, resting his cigarette between his lips as he looks me up and down, his gaze lingering on the swell of my breasts in my tight mini dress. "It's a nasty habit."

"Why not quit?"

"I don't want to," he deadpans, a slight rasp to his already low, smoky voice.

I lick my lips, unsure what to say next. There's tension between us. I've felt it since the moment I met him for the first time. It's electric, dangerous, and delicious. It's everything it shouldn't be.

"I thought you were spending the night in NOLA." He takes another step toward me, close enough I can smell the leather of his jacket and the slightly musky spice of his skin.

"Well, obviously I'm not."

"Why?"

"Why do you care?"

"Because now you're walking barefoot in the dark."

"Well, you're creeping around in the dark. What's the difference?"

"I'm not creeping around–"

"Stalking me, then?" My words were supposed to be a playful little jab, but I say them with more force than I mean to.

Dalton's mouth ticks up at the edges into a cocky smile, his eyes the shade of raw, uncut emeralds in the slices of moonlight drifting between the branches overhead. His tongue darts out, slowly pressing against the inside of his lower lip. "Why do I feel like you're going to be disappointed when I tell you I'm not stalking you, Angel?"

"I don't believe you."

He stares down at me, slowly bringing his cigarette to his lips. His throat tightens as he takes a long, exaggerated drag and lets the smoke fall from his lips. "I don't think you want to believe me. I think you like the thrill, Layla, of being hunted."

Chills lick up and down my spine, settling low in my belly. He searches my eyes and smirks.

"I knew it."

"Knew what?"

He walks past me toward the house.

"I knew you were kind of fucked up. You'd have to be to take a night shift at this place."

I whirl toward him, chasing after him. "I'm not fucked up!"

"What would you call it, then?" He stops walking, stubbing out his cigarette with the toe of his shoe and looks down at me expectantly.

I curl my hands into fists at my sides, gripping the straps of my heels like a weapon. His gaze sweeps over me, slow and thoughtful, like he's drinking me in. Again, he lingers on my breasts.

"Take a fucking picture, Dalton. It'll last longer."

"Oh, don't tempt me," he rasps, taking a single step toward me, which effectively closes the distance between us. "Say the word, and I'll do you one better and paint you naked, Angel. Every curve."

I find it hard to catch my breath as his words brush over my cheek. Another step and he's mere inches away, his body casting mine in his shadow. He chuckles to himself as he runs his knuckles over my chest, his fingertips grazing the low neckline that does nothing to hide my cleavage.

My nipples peak, aching to be felt. I hate that his touch ignites a fire within me that pools between my thighs.

What's worse is that he notices the way I melt, and his eyes darken, his expression shifting from feline amusement to something dripping with hunger, maybe even desire. When I don't immediately shy away from his touch, he smooths his hand up my side, caressing my left breast.

I don't dare take a breath. I just stand there, stupidly, letting this perfect stranger touch me.

His eyes don't leave mine for a single second as he hooks his thumb under the top of my dress and tugs down.

The flimsy fabric rips, the sound echoing around us. It's enough to break me from whatever trance he put me under.

I swing my heels by the straps, aiming for his head, but with a dark chuckle he backs out of my range of motion.

But to my surprise, he doesn't retreat. He stalks toward me and rips the shoes from my hands and presses me up against a tree. "Hey! Get off!"

"Do not come out here alone at night again," he commands, his voice dropping to something low and fierce, a tone that sends ripples of fear through my body.

I squirm, trying to get out of his grasp, but he clutches my arms and shoves me back against the tree. "Dalton!"

He releases me, stepping back, his expression unreadable. He points to the house. "Go."

I sniff indignantly, brushing bark and dirt from my ass and thighs. I almost tell him to fuck off, but the look on his face makes me want to shrivel up and die.

"Go to the house, now."

"You act like the *boogeyman* is out here hunting me, Dalton!"

"I'm not entirely sure he isn't."

I keep my eyes on his until I pass him. His footsteps behind me fill the air around us until we finally reach the house. He tosses my shoes toward the screen door. "Go to bed."

"Who do you think you are?" I whirl to face him.

"You're drunk, Layla. Did that man who picked you up earlier really drop you off at the gate and make you walk–"

"I got a ride back here, asshole. And, Adam? Bailey's cousin?" I step toward him. "You were watching me when I left, weren't you?"

He tucks his hands in the pockets of his jacket.

"You were. You watched me leave." I advance on him, closing the distance between us. "Were you at the club tonight, Dalton?"

His steely expression shifts, his mouth quirking up at the corners. "Why would I have gone to a nightclub in New Orleans, Layla?"

"I don't know. Were you there?"

"I don't know where *there* is–"

"Did you come up behind me and–and–" I can barely finish the sentence. "Touch me."

A muscle in his jaw ticks, but his eyes give nothing away. "Sounds like you had a grand old time, but not with me. You would've known it was me touching you, Angel, because you would've been screaming my fucking name."

"Fuck you," I snarl, and walk to the house, throwing open the screen door. Deciding I'm not done railing on him yet, I turn back, but the driveway is dark and empty.

That fucking dickhead probably ran along the side of the house to get away from me. Good. Fuck him, anyway. I stumble into the quiet house. It's probably 2:00 in the morning. I'm not actually sure. In fact, I'm pretty sure Bailey has my purse, which is just fantastic, and I also think I must have left my phone in the backseat of the Uber.

"God damnit," I hiss as I trudge up the stairs. A light is on in my aunt's room. Vera is probably still awake tending to her, so I don't bother checking on Aunt Penny. I'm off until Monday, anyway.

My room is cool and dark, shadows dancing in every corner like usual. The curtains drift with the soft breeze coming through the screened windows, the song of cicadas filling the room.

I lean against the door and close my eyes, trying to calm my racing heart.

Part of me wants to go find Dalton and give him another piece of my mind. The other part of me wants to find him and let him paint me naked like he offered. Or, more likely, threatened. I groan, sinking into a crouch and resting my face in my hands.

I can still feel his touch on my skin and smell his smokey, spicy scent as I get out of the shower sometime later and fall naked into bed. My fingers immediately drift between my thighs, gliding through the wetness pooled there.

And while I tease myself, I imagine it's Dalton's thumb circling my clit. I imagine his mouth on my neck and his taste on my tongue. I imagine it's him nudging my legs apart, and his cock dragging over my pussy before pressing inside of me.

Something about him has me conflicted. I don't like him. I think he's mean, honestly. I think he's rude and trying to scare me for some reason.

But after tonight, I also know my body craves his touch.

I fall asleep, and the last whimpered word on my lips is his name.

11

DALTON

I SHOULD THROTTLE HER. That's exactly what I should have done when I had her pressed against that tree. She's either completely dense or truly fearless.

I honestly don't know which is worse.

Walking around the property at night is not something I'll allow her to do again, even if it means keeping her chained to her bed. God, the thought of her tied up and at my mercy makes my balls tighten as I stalk around the side of the house toward the detached garage. I throw the door open, forcing the image of Layla naked and prone, her eyes heavy with desire, out of my mind.

The garage is cool and dark as I close the door behind me. No one here uses the garage but me. I keep my old truck here, tucked out of sight. I reach through the open passenger window and grab the bottle of scotch I picked up earlier tonight and wrench the lid open. Leaning against the side of my truck, I take a drink. Then another, and another, until I've finished off at least a quarter of the bottle. The scotch curls through my veins, slowing the thundering beats of my heart to a crawl as I sink to the ground.

I should just drink until I pass out, which, admittedly, was the reason I came out here for that bottle instead of going back inside with Layla.

But running into her during a walk up and down the half-mile long driveway has me entirely on edge.

If it hadn't been me out there, it would have been someone else. And she wouldn't be tucked in bed right now. I would have found her half rotted corpse in the marsh a few weeks from now instead.

I take another drink as the memory of the last night nurse comes to mind. Abigale, twenty-eight, beautiful and kind. God, the house wanted her. It hunted her in a way I'd never seen before. I left her alone; she had no idea I was even in the house, but that was my mistake.

Abigail is rotting somewhere in the marsh now, I'm sure.

I close my eyes and finish off half the bottle before peeling myself from the floor and walking back out into the darkness, letting the night swirl around me. Layla's phone–which I'd found face down on the driveway near the front gate, buzzes in my pocket. I meant to give it back to her when I caught up to her earlier, but the thought completely slipped my mind. I'll leave it somewhere in the house for her to find in the morning.

But Layla's bedroom light is still on when I slip through the back door. Vera is sitting at the kitchen table with her back turned to me as I walk with silent steps through the kitchen. She balances a slim cigarette on her red-painted lips, her eyes locked on her magazine. She doesn't see me, and instead of leaving Layla's phone by the coffee machine like I intended, I decide I might as well deliver it upstairs for her.

That incessant scratching sound echoes through the house as I round a corner and walk into the foyer. Shadows dance in the formal living room, and for a split second I'm sure I see a young woman sitting at the grand piano, her ghostly white fingers resting on the keys. I take another drink from the bottle and let the booze snake through my body, numbing my senses, the same senses that allow me to see these things–these ghosts. This house is full of them.

They don't care about me. They're not bothered by my presence. But one of them….

That scratching sound rakes over my skin, setting my blood on fire. There's nothing I can take or drink that will let me sleep through it, not tonight.

Not after I learned something, *someone*, followed Layla to New Orleans.

Someone she thought was me touched her, and that thought has me stalking up the stairs toward her room.

Call it possessive, call it an obsession, I don't give a fuck. I made it perfectly clear who this one belonged to, and *that's me*.

Her door is unlocked again. I slip inside with ease, closing the door behind me and turning the lock. A near silent click whispers through the air.

Her bedside lamp is on, but otherwise, the room is cast in inky black shadows. I look around, assuring myself that I'm alone, then let my gaze rest on her naked body.

Naked, she's lying on her side, one of her hands pinched between her upper thighs. Her mouth is parted, her brow furrowed as her breasts rise and fall with each breath. A soft whimper leaves her lips, and her expression relaxes.

She's dreaming again.

I lean against the door and watch her as I take another pull from the bottle of scotch, nearly finishing it off. Layla squeezes her thighs together, her brow furrowing. The wetness pooled between her fingers glimmers in the lamplight. She lets out a soft moan that has my senses on high alert.

Fuck me. I shouldn't be in here watching her do this. I shouldn't be in here at all, actually. Instead of leaving, I take another drink and set the empty bottle on the table by the door, my eyes still locked on her hand as she fingers herself in her sleep.

The sheets are bunched at her feet as I slowly approach the bed, resting my fists against the mattress. She smells like honeysuckle and vanilla—like a warm summer day when all the flowers are in bloom, their scent carried by a cool breeze. Her golden hair falls in tendrils over her shoulders—like pure silk, glistening with an amber sheen in the lamplight. I imagine the way I'd paint her hair, the colors I'd use to create that precious gold woven with streaks of warm platinum. Her skin is the color of pale honey, tan and freckled from the sun. I reach for her, my fingers hovering just above her skin, imagining how warm and supple she'd be to touch.

"Dalton."

I arch my brows as my name leaves her lips. I wasn't expecting that. I'm not sure what I'd been expecting when I came in here. I think I was hoping she'd be awake so she could fight with me some more, but this… this is so much better.

I slowly crawl onto the bed and get on my knees beside her. My fingertips wander softly over her skin.

She lets out a breath slowly as I smooth my hand down the length of her arm in a featherlight touch. Her eyes remain closed as I run my knuckles over the curve of her bare waist and over her hip bone, the flat of her belly, and down to where her hand is still covering her sex.

"Dalton," she moans, and arches her beautiful, slender neck. I fixate on the artery there, on the way the blood is rushing through it, wondering how fast her heart is beating right now.

I slowly, carefully, guide her onto her back.

I could have my way with her, right here, right now. She's a hard sleeper, and the movement doesn't wake her up in the slightest, but her body reacts to my touch as I slide my hands up her waist, relishing in how the fine, white, downy hair on her arms prickles and stands on end, her rosy nipples hardening.

I straddle her legs but lift up enough so that we're not touching. She arches her hips like she's trying to find me, desperate for the pressure of my body against hers.

I called her fucked up earlier, and I meant it. I would know because I'm just as fucked up as she is. I'm fucked up enough to be here, in her room, touching her while she's asleep. And she's fucked up enough to be dreaming about me while touching herself.

It takes all of my willpower not to strip off my jeans and press my aching cock into the sweet, tight pussy that's beckoning to me with each whimpering breath she takes. When her hands reach out to me, I gently pin her wrists to the bed on either side of her thighs, and lean down, brushing my lips over her ear, her jaw, and her neck. Her chest rises, her breasts trembling as she inhales sharply. She whispers my name again like a prayer, a nearly silent plea. I wonder what I'm doing to her in her dream. I'd love to see inside her mind for just a moment, long enough to confirm I'm making her beg.

Her hips shift from side to side beneath me as I lower my head and blow on each nipple, then release one of her wrists and slide my fingers through her wet folds. I stifle the groan that threatens to leave my lips as I plunge my fingers inside of her, her walls tightening around me.

She makes a choked sound, a soft whimpered moan, and clamps her lips together. I freeze, watching her beautiful face.

She starts moving against my touch, desperate to create that friction she needs to come.

"Happy to oblige," I whisper, the only sound I've made so far, and then I fuck her with my fingers until she's arching that sweet ass off the bed and crying out my name to the ceiling.

When I'm through, I tuck her in tight, and her body relaxes back into what I hope is deep, dreamless rest. The kind of sleep reserved for the dead is what she needs more than anything, and what the house refuses to allow her. I'll come here every night if I have to, just for this, just to see her silent and still with the sheets tucked tight around her curves and the moonlight playing over her peaceful face.

I turn off the lamp and edge off the bed with every intention of grabbing the bottle of scotch on my way out, but stop, my fingers curled around the neck.

I leave it on the table by the door knowing it'll be the first thing she sees when she wakes up in the morning. She'll wonder what happened, wonder who has been here and why.

If anything, maybe she'll realize she's not alone in this.

I sit on the stool in my studio sometime later, the sun finally beginning its journey over the horizon.

"I warned you about going after this one," I say to the room while dabbing a paintbrush on the palate resting in my lap. "She's mine. Don't test me."

12

Layla

I know I'm in a dream.

The room around me is all white—creamy white curtains drifting in a phantom breeze, white walls glistening with warm sunshine. It feels like I'm out of my own body as Dalton lowers his head, his incredible green eyes shining like smooth jade. I wrap my arms around his neck while his lips hover over mine.

He's close enough I could kiss him. I want to. I wonder what he tastes like more than anything.

"Tell me what you want, Angel."

"I want you," I whisper, trailing my fingertips over the back of his neck.

"Eyes on me," he whispers, then lowers his head. I feel the briefest featherlight touch of his lips against my own before the dream disintegrates and I'm yanked back to startling reality.

Naked and tangled in sweaty, damp sheets, I sit up and rub my eyes. My head throbs as the memories of last night come rushing back to me.

Gin. I'd been drinking gin. I'd also been day drinking and ordered a mimosa at practically every cafe we explored before even thinking about checking out New Orleans's night scene. Then, back in Hahnville, I'd stumbled out of the Uber and walked back to the house where Dalton had met me halfway down the driveway.

The memory of him almost tugging my dress down and exposing my breasts–the thought of him touching me so intimately in general–has my skin prickling with the need to be touched.

I'm on dangerous ground with him, I realize. There's obviously something heated brewing between us, and this could get out of hand.

Do I want to fuck him? Uh, hell yeah. Especially now that the man haunts my dreams almost every night. Is falling into bed with him a good idea?

Absolutely not.

I know with every fiber of my being that Dalton is the kind of guy that could fuck up my life. He'd fuck me like a god and then disappear. I'd wear our encounter like a scar for the rest of my life.

My phone buzzes on the bedside table. I blink into the sunlight and reach for it, shocked to learn it's nearly noon already. I swear I left it in the Uber…. Maybe I was more drunk last night than I thought.

Thank God it's Sunday, and I have the day, and night, off.

I flop back against the pillows and stare up at the ceiling. I'm sticky with sweat, and the stifling heat of the day has already warmed the room past the point of being comfortable. But, I have nothing to do. No plans, nowhere to go, nowhere to be.

My phone rings, and I pick it up, squinting at the screen for a moment before answering it.

"Hey–"

"Hey! I'm just making sure you're okay!" Bailey's voice echoes through the phone.

I wince, the volume sending my already aching head throbbing anew. "I'm totally fine. I just drank way more than I realized and felt pretty sick."

"Well, I'm glad you got home all right. You could drive out and meet us back in NOLA if you want. I'm not going back to Hahnville until later tonight."

"I'm gonna stay here. You were right about me needing to catch up on sleep."

"Did you just wake up?" She laughs, her voice like soft music.

"Yeah, I did." I smile to myself as her laughter fills my ears. I turn my head toward my bedroom door while Bailey gives me the rundown about the rest of the night, how she danced with some guys from the club until the early hours of the morning, and how Adam and Carlos went to brunch without her this morning.

But as she talks--and talks, and talks--I'm barely listening, unaware of most of her words because I'm staring at an empty bottle of scotch on the side table next to my bedroom door.

A single rose sticks out of the top, its blood red petals shimmering in the sunlight.

"Bailey," I say after I find my voice again. "Do you know much about Dalton?"

The line between us fizzles and cracks, the call momentarily breaking up. "What did you say? I can barely hear you?"

"Dalton," I repeat, slowly sitting up with my eyes locked on the bottle of scotch. "The artist who lives here."

"Who? Layla–"

The call abruptly drops. My phone slips out of my hand as I stare at the bottle. One of the petals falls from the rose, fluttering down to land on the table without a sound.

I'm out of bed in an instant. I pull on a shirt and shorts then storm barefoot out of my room and hurtle down the stairs, skipping the last few steps.

Dalton is nowhere to be found on the first floor or the second. I even open the door to Aunt Penny's room, where Vera is sitting in the chair reading a magazine. She glares at me, shooting daggers with her eyes as I shut the door and continue looking in each and every room on the second floor.

Reluctantly, I walk up the creaking staircase to the third floor and begin yanking on every door I come across.

Everything is locked, and I didn't bring the keys.

The fourth floor is the same, and I don't spend a second more than I have to up there. It's the one untouched floor of the house. The wood floor is caked in dust and grime from decades of neglect. "Dalton?" I say into the damp, dust filled air.

The creaking, scratching sound answers me, right above my head where the attic rests.

I sprint away like my life depends on it, almost falling down the stairs leading from the third floor, and race down the narrow, darkened hallway until I reach the flight of stairs leading to the second floor, then the first.

Vera is in the supply room now. She turns, shouting, "Nurse Bryant! What on earth are you doing?!"

I skid to a stop in the foyer, panting, my sleep ruffled hair standing on end as I fight for breath. "Where the hell is Dalton?"

"Who?" she asks, blinking at me with a scowl pinching her thin brows together.

"Dalton," I pant, throwing her an exasperated look. "The boarder."

She rolls her eyes and turns back to whatever she was doing. "I don't see anyone else here. Do you?" She turns and gives me a look that makes me assume she thinks I've lost my mind.

I huff out a breath and run my hands over my face before walking toward the kitchen. She's just fucking with me to be mean. I make a pot of coffee, tapping my nails on the counter while I wait for it to brew. That creepy motherfucker left me a rose, didn't he? How long was he in my room? And what, exactly, was he doing while he was there?

I slip on a pair of sandals I leave in the kitchen, and I'm out the back door the second I have a mug of coffee in my hand, stomping down the steps. I walk for a while, unsure of where I'm going. All I know is that I need to get out of the house--now. I walk until I reach the tree line where Curtis's immaculate landscaping ends and the wild marshlands begin.

It's strangely noisy here. Insects buzz and chirp, and a breeze rustles the leaves overhead. In the distance, I can see the slight rise of the old cemetery. The marsh hugs it, creating what I can only describe as a small island, the murky water surrounding the headstones shimmering in the sunlight.

I lift my coffee to my lips to finally take a sip but catch movement out of the corner of my eye. A tall, dark haired man is walking through the marsh, his back to me. His outfit is... strange. Old and out of place. He looks like he just stepped out of one of the BBC dramas my mom loves to watch.

"Dalton!" I screech, my temper flaring. Dalton—and I'm sure it's him—continues to walk through the trees until he disappears from sight. Fuck. I chug my coffee and toss the mug behind me before stepping across the boundary of the backyard into the wild marsh beyond.

It's much cooler out here in the shade of the trees. I carefully walk in the direction I saw Dalton headed in, dressed in his weird outfit. Maybe he's into historical reenactments? LARPing? Who knows, but that's not what's important right now. I grumble curses as I maneuver through the woods which eventually gives way to the marsh. Soon I'm ankle deep in water, and can't see the house behind me anymore.

"DALTON!" I cry out. My voice is absorbed by the sounds of the swamp, disappearing into a flurry of birdsong and the flapping of wings. I instinctively cover my head as several large birds I can't identify erupt in flight behind me, squawking with alarm. "Jesus Christ," I groan. "Where the hell am I?"

I've lost Dalton at this point. He had to know I was screaming his name, right? Surely he wouldn't just leave me out here. Or, this was his plan all along, and now he's got me alone and vulnerable.

I stalk forward, unsure which direction I'm traveling in now. My sandals catch in the muddy bottom of the marsh as I fight my way toward a thicket of trees that looks like it's situated on a rise. My priorities shift from tracking down Dalton to getting out of the marsh and back on dry land. What had I been thinking?

Finally, I haul myself out of the marsh and make my way through the trees. It is, in fact, a slope, and in a few minutes, I'm cresting a small bluff with a sweeping view of the marshlands beyond.

The cemetery is only a few hundred yards away, by my estimation. If I can get there, it's a straight shot back to the house, but it means trudging through the marsh that encircles it again.

I blink into the sunlight, which is absolutely roasting me. Wiping sweat from my brow, I pant, and start my journey to the cemetery.

"Fuck you, Dalton," I groan ten minutes later. I'm wet to the knees, my legs covered in mud, and my sandals are absolutely trashed. My hair falls over my shoulders–sticking to my face and neck. It has to be close to a hundred degrees right now, and there's no breeze over here. Not at all.

I grunt with effort as I wade through another stretch of marsh water and reach a set of decaying stone steps. The hair on the back of my neck rises as I step out of the water and look around, noticing headstones partly submerged in the swamp, the visible stone covered in algae and moss.

I shiver at the thought of the sheer number of graves I've just walked over to get here.

But, thank God, I can finally see the house again, and I know exactly what route I need to take to get back home.

Tired and overheated, I sink into a crouch and rest my elbows on my knees, closing my eyes against the relentless glare of the hot summer sun. I've almost forgotten why I came out here in the first place when I open my eyes again, and something red catches my attention.

At the crest of the small hill, an unkempt and severely overgrown rose bush snakes between a trio of headstones. It's in full bloom and smells divine in contrast to the rank stench of the stagnant water all around me. A cold sweat breaks out along my hairline as I slowly raise my head and peer at the blood red rose blooms.

That fucker not only left me a rose, but he'd picked it here... in the cemetery.

I struggle to my feet, my legs aching from my trek through the marsh, and walk to the rose bush, brushing my fingers over the satin-like petals. I reach to pluck a particular perfect rose from its stem when a shadow looms over me.

My scream barely leaves my throat before I'm yanked away and whirled around, my wet, muddy sandals sliding over the overgrown grass.

13

DALTON

LAYLA'S COVERED head to toe in mud. She looks absolutely feral, and the fear and confusion in her eyes is notable as she loses her footing and falls right into my arms.

Arm, actually. I keep my sketchbook raised above my head to prevent the mud and grime she's plastered in from spilling onto the pages of fresh sketches I've been working on all morning.

My other arm is roped around her waist as I haul her to her feet. She staggers backward, her mud laden sandals sliding off her feet. "D-Dalton!"

"Layla?" I laugh, unable to help it. "What are you doing out here?"

She screws her face into a scowl, her cheeks the color of ripe tomatoes, before she explodes, "I followed you, you fucking dickhead!"

"Me? Why?"

She looks me up and down, her expression shifting from outright fury to something I can only describe as utter bewilderment. "What happened to your costume?"

"My what?" I set my sketchpad on top of one of the headstones and take off my hat, running my fingers through my hair before securing the paint stained, faded baseball cap back on my head.

"Your costume."

I look down at my outfit, which is nothing more than a gray T-shirt I've had since high school and tan Carhartt pants. My rubber boots come nearly to my knees. "What the hell are you talking about, Layla?" I scan her face then reach out to touch the top of her head, looking for bumps, to make sure she hasn't fucking collapsed and given herself a concussion.

She shoves me off, scowling up at me, her white teeth bared in a snarl. "You were dressed like you were going to a Civil War reen-actment!"

"Uh… are you okay? How long have you been out here?" I take my backpack off and start unzipping it, reaching for the jug of water I brought out with me this morning. "Drink this."

"I'm not drinking anything you offer me! It's probably drugged!"

"What the hell is wrong with you right now?"

She's sunburned and obviously soaking wet up to her waist. Her thin shorts were once light blue but are now a slimy green color and splattered with mud. Her shirt is no better, and beads of sweat roll down her temples as she huffs and puffs at me.

"Layla," I say, slowly, carefully. "What's wrong?"

"What's wrong? You're asking me what's wrong?"

I'm beginning to wonder if she's having heat stroke when she edges closer to me, yanking the water jug she's just refused out of my hands and wrenching it open. I watch her take several long, desperate drinks of the cold water, her cheeks flushing.

She wipes her mouth and shoves the water into my chest, backing away. "You were in my room last night. You left an empty bottle of booze with a rose in it on the table by my door."

"I didn't leave you a rose." I say nothing about the bottle, but she knows I did that, judging by the furious look in her eyes.

"So you admit you were in my room?"

I arch my brow at her. This conversation could go two ways, and

I'm not sure which way I'd enjoy more. Her feathers are already ruffled as it is, and while I'd love to cage her in and tell her I'd thoroughly enjoyed running my hands up and down the length of her naked body while she cried out my name in her sleep, I decide to focus on the fact she looks like she's about to pass out from heat exhausted and delirium instead.

"You need to come with me back to the house," I hedge, extending a hand to her. "It's dangerous out here, and you're not dressed to be exploring the marsh, especially alone."

Her lower lip juts out. God damnit, the pout she's giving me right now could bring me to my knees.

"Layla–"

"If you didn't leave me a rose, who did?"

"I don't know. But I *was* in your room."

"Why?"

"I was checking on you. You were shitfaced last night and dropped your phone at the gate. Our little… fight made me forget I had it until you were already in the house."

She blushes, her face turning a new fiery shade of red I'd love to capture in a painting. "What did you see?" she asks, her voice dropping to a mere whisper. Embarrassment flashes behind her sapphire eyes as she meekly meets my gaze.

"A lot," I admit, a touch wryly. "But don't worry. I don't plan on telling anyone about your wet dreams–"

"I wasn't–"

I cut her off with an arch of my brow. She purses her lips and looks down at her muddy feet. Her arms come around her waist, and that's when I see it. Blood. I take her left hand and hold it up to the sun. "You got yourself pretty good," I say, examining the wound on her wrist.

"It was the rose bush," she says with a shrug, then winces and draws in a breath as I graze my thumb over the long, jagged scratch.

"You need to clean it out really well. This place is filthy."

"Why are you out here, then?"

I meet her eyes, unaccustomed to her soft, conversational tone. I run my thumb over her wrist again, finding the place where I can feel her heart rate, which is faster than I expected. "I came out here to work on some sketches. The wall paper in the cigar room is all local flora, a lot of which can be found out here if you know where to look." I search her eyes for a moment. "I wasn't walking around in Civil War garb, Layla."

"I swear I saw you. I followed you and ended up way out in the middle of the marsh."

I lick my lips, still holding her wrist. "Don't do that again." The words are a steady, but harsh, warning. Her eyes shine with an understanding neither of us voices right away.

Finally, she asks, "I saw a ghost, didn't I?"

"Possibly. Have you ever seen one before?"

She looks almost embarrassed.

"It's fine if you have," I say, edging a little closer to her, my thumb traveling back over her wrist as I drop my gaze to her skin, to the blood beginning to drip from her wound. "I see them too."

She looks up at me, startled. "You do?"

"All the time."

Her chest rises and falls as she holds my gaze. "Are you not afraid?"

"No," I tell her firmly. Her eyes glimmer as I raise her wrist to my lips and press a kiss to her wound, her blood staining my lips. "Nothing here is going to hurt you." It's a lie, unless I can find a way to run her out of this place before it's too late. But now, standing in the middle of the Gregory family cemetery, her skin pressed against my lips, the only thing I can think about is how badly I want her to stay.

Isn't this how all the other men who'd stayed in this house went mad?

Her lips part, and she exhales sharply from the sting as I run the tip of my tongue over her wound. The metallic taste of her blood sings through my mouth, igniting that heat that has plagued me since last night.

"Dalton?"

"Yes, Angel?"

She takes several ragged breaths as I back her against one of the headstones, caging her in, letting go of her wrist. I have to lean down to kiss her. She's incredibly short, barely taller than the headstone at her back. I know once my lips touch hers there will be repercussions for both of us, and the menace that led her into the marsh will not be happy about it.

It only makes me want to kiss her more.

When she rises up on her toes to meet me, I brush my lips over hers in a featherlight touch. I feel her hands grip my shirt, her knuckles digging into my abdomen. She wants this bad. I can feel it; I can almost taste her need as I barely press my lips to hers.

She tastes like coffee with a minty, fresh undertone reminiscent of toothpaste. I smile despite myself, and run my tongue along her lower lip, urging her to open up to me so I can explore her mouth further. But just as she does, and a breathy little moan escapes her throat, I pull away.

"Let's go."

She scoffs, her beautiful eyes narrowing on mine.

"Come on back to the house."

"Why did you…. You're teasing me."

I shrug, "Is there something else you want from me, Layla?" My voice is smooth and heavy, dripping with desire I can't stifle in the moment.

She takes another breath, and that artery in her throat jumps as her heart rate flutters.

I lean forward again, closing the distance between us. Brushing my words over her cheek, I whisper, "I will do anything your heart desires. You just have to tell me what you want, and where you want it. Do you want me on my knees, Angel? Do you want me to pull those little shorts down and take you from behind, right here, against a headstone? How sick is that dirty mind of yours, Layla, tell me. Tell me about that dream you had last night."

She pulls away, swallowing hard, her cheeks flaming red.

I straighten up, chuckling to myself. "Thought so."

"You thought what?" she snaps just as I turn away from her and start walking down the crest of the hill. "Dalton!"

"If you need relief, come find me. In the meantime, get your ass back to the house. You need to take care of that scratch before it gets infected."

She huffs out a breath and mumbles something to herself, likely a curse on my name, but follows me away from the cemetery regardless. I choose a direct, mostly dry, path, not that it matters at this rate. She's already coated in the muck that floats on top of the marsh. When we reach the cypress trees, she blows past me, kicking her muddy sandals off in the yard before running toward the back porch.

"Don't even think about it!" I snap, pointing to the water house.

She glares at me with her fingers curled around the railing of the steps before hopping back down and walking with determination to the water hose.

14

LAYLA

I WATCH Dalton disappear around the side of the house. My heart is still pounding in my chest as I rinse off my legs with the hose and stand in the sun to dry off for a moment. My wrist throbs where I sliced it open on the rose bush. That, or from the feeling of Dalton's tongue gliding over my skin, which had felt… electrifying.

I blush, then blow out my breath, wiping my wet, bare feet on the grass. I pick up my sandals and the mug I'd tossed in the yard before my ill-fated journey through the marsh and walk into the quiet house. I'm not sure where Dalton went, but after dumping my muddy sandals in the utility sink in the laundry room and walking up to my room, I gather he's not in the house.

I take a cold shower, scrubbing what feels like years' worth of grime from my skin. I scrub and scrub until my skin is raw and aching and then wrap myself in a towel and sit on the edge of my bed in the hot sun to fully dry.

Dark clouds form in the distance, and the smell of oncoming rain seeps through the window screen as I brush my wet hair and dress in soft, comfy linen pajamas. It's only 3:00 in the afternoon, but I have the night off again. I need to stay on my night schedule, however, so I slide into bed and take a nap.

Sometime later, I wake to a storm thundering overhead and rain pooling on the windowsills where it seeps through the old sealant. I'm woken fully by a sharp jolt of lightning that lights up my room with a startling flash of blue. The power flickers. I reach for my phone, realizing I hadn't put it on the charger, and it's sitting at two percent battery. It's also nearly ten o'clock. I've slept the entire day away.

Another flicker of my bedside lamp steals my attention just in time for the power in the house to cut out entirely.

"Oh, shit," I exclaim, nearly falling out of bed and rushing toward my door. Vera's footsteps are already echoing in the corridor when I pull it open and step out into the dark hallway.

I follow Vera into my aunt's room. An unsettling kind of silence seeps through the walls. I'm so used to the soft beeps of her ECG machine keeping me company at night, and now there's nothing but her soft exhales and the fluttering of the curtains. Rain slams in silver sheets against the windows as thunder and lightning crack the sky in two above us.

I walk to Vera's side as she checks on my aunt, a flashlight pinched between her teeth as she examines Aunt Penny's IV port on her wrist. Vera backs away, clutching the flashlight, and turns to me. "She's fine without the ECG. It does nothing but monitor her heart rate."

"I know," I tell her, not liking her mocking tone. "Do we not have a backup generator? I'm more worried about the cameras in here–"

"I'm still on shift until tomorrow morning," Vera snaps, crossing her arms. "You have no reason to even be in here, Nurse Bryant. I have it handled."

I bristle at her tone, straightening my shoulders just a touch. "I'm just–"

"Go downstairs and take care of that hand of yours," she says, cutting me off with a little wave of the flashlight. "There's a lantern inside the dumbwaiter by the stairs. Take that with you. I'll stay here with her."

Another flash of lightning illuminates the old woman's face.

"Fine, just keep me updated on her–"

"Goodnight," Vera snaps.

I hiss out a breath and storm out of the room. The house creaks and shutters as the storm rages overhead. I look up at the ceiling, seeing nothing but shadows. It's so dark. So eerily quiet. I find myself holding my breath until my fingers curl around the handle of the battery powered lantern and slam the creepy dumbwaiter shut, pressing myself against the wall as I fumble with the on switch.

The lantern sends a flare of flickering light through the stairwell as I creep downstairs, my footsteps creaking with each step. Without power, the lantern is the only way to guide my steps, but the faint glow also creates intense, fluttering shadows that make me want to crawl out of my skin and find somewhere to hide.

In the total, all-consuming darkness, I should feel utterly alone.

But I don't. I've never felt truly alone in this house.

I stumble into the supply room and root through boxes of gauze and bandages, fumbling in the dark. My wrist has been throbbing since I woke up, the skin around the jagged scrape puffy with irritation. I rip a length of tape with my teeth and spread my goodies out on the plastic work table in the center of the room. Alcohol, bacitracin, the works. I chew my lip as I quickly clean the wound and wrap it in clean bandages, wincing at the sharp sting from the alcohol.

I have it in mind to break into the sharps to find some penicillin, just to be on the safe side, when the lantern flickers and cuts out, casting me in pure, soul sucking blackness.

I freeze. "Shit," I whisper, inhaling sharply. I slowly run my hand over the table, looking for the lantern. "Shit, shit, shit."

Lightning pierces the sky, filling the room with a brief burst of light. A male figure comes into view near the window for a split second before we're swept into total darkness again.

"Dalton?" I blink attempting to clear my vision enough to see past my fingertips as I stretch my hand across the table.

"If you'd only accepted my rose, you might not have scratched your beautiful wrist on that hedge in the cemetery." His voice sounds far away, like there are miles between us, yet it wraps itself around me and drags me down under what feels like fathoms of water. He doesn't sound like himself. His voice lacks that dry, sarcastic edge.

But it's him. Who else could it be? His sudden presence in the room is overwhelming, but strangely... unfamiliar.

"You told me you weren't the one who left me the rose," I say, my voice straining over each word.

My skin prickles when a soft ripple of air brushes over my arms, then my neck, like he's standing behind me now. "You are like a rose, my pet. Soft and supple. Stealing the beauty of every flower around you." Each word brushes over my skin, but it's cold. Draining. My skin prickles with adrenaline as my heart begins to race.

Not with need. Not with that feral desire.

With fear.

I whirl around as thunder crashes, sending a shudder through the room. "I d-don't like this game," I tell him. "Th-this is too far."

"Do you not like the dreams I've sent you?" He's behind me again, like he's moving soundlessly around me.

"Go away–"

"Did you not love the way I touched you while you slept?"

I suck in a surprised breath as that cold rush of air sweeps over me again, chilling me to the bone.

Another flash of lightning casts the room in ribbons of blue, slicing through the shadows.

He's in front of me, only a few feet away. But the lightning travels through him like he's one of the shadows dancing in each corner of the room.

I know, without an ounce of a doubt, that this isn't Dalton. Whatever it is might look like him, might sound like him, but it's not him. *It's not him.* It's something else.

I take a step away, my back hitting the shelves with a crunch that sends an ache down my spine.

"Are you afraid, pet?"

Pet. Not Angel.

I can sense him coming closer. My mind spins as I try to make sense of this situation, but I find myself falling into a state of delirium.

"I'm dreaming," I say out loud. "This is another dream." It would make sense. Have I not had dreams just like this one, where the voice is familiar but somehow wrong?

"Come to me, Layla."

"N-no–"

"Submit."

"No, I won't."

A dark, cackling laugh cuts through the air. His voice rings through the room like a death knell. "I will have you, one way or another. *I always do.*"

When lightning flashes again, I see him clearly for the first time. His face–it's sharper, more... maddening. It's like looking at Dalton through his reflection in the mirror and the angles are all wrong. The way his lips tick up in a smile is all wrong. And his eyes? They're not the soft, polished jade I've come to find familiar. They're black pits of the same sucking darkness choking the room.

"No," I say with more force. "This is a dream. A nightmare." I squeeze my eyes shut and dig my nails into my arms, hugging myself tight. *Wake up. Wake up. Wake up!*

"Layla..." My name is whispered over my cheek. It's enough to break me from my fear fueled stupor.

I run, tripping over the rug in the foyer and falling to my knees. I flail in the dark, finding my grip on the very first step on the stairs.

"Layla..."

I choke on a silent scream as I tear up the stairs. "Leave me alone!"

The second floor is silent and dark and feels like it stretches for miles as I tear down the corridor and wrench on my aunt's door. The door finally gives way and opens so abruptly that I fall inside, landing on my knees.

"Vera–" I open my eyes and gape at the empty room. It spans out in front of me, dust hanging in the lightning fueled haze that illuminates cobwebs and furniture covered in rotting sheets.

My breath catches in my throat as I slowly turn my head to where Aunt Penny's bed rests. I clasp my hands to my mouth as she stares down at me, her face withering to the bone with each passing second.

This is a dream. This is all a dream.

But my name echoes through the air. His voice carries an unfamiliar lilt as it travels down the hallway outside of Aunt Penny's room. He's coming. He'll be here any moment.

I'm up in a split second, backing out of the room, tears falling down my cheeks. I stumble back into the hallway unsure of which direction I'm facing.

"Layla! *You cannot hide from me...*"

I feel along the wall for my own door, but the wall stretches on and on, completely smooth. I can't find the door. I'm growing more frantic as I glide down the wall, sending silent prayers to whatever gods are listening to *help me.*

"LAYLA!" Dalton's voice booms through the hallway, murderous and full of rage.

"Leave me alone!"

A sharp scratching sound erupts all around me, like nails against a chalkboard. My ears ring, the noise blurring my senses as I break into a sprint through the inky darkness. Thunder continues to shatter the sky, each boom settling in my bones. I should have woken up by now. I keep pinching myself and running into the wall, scraping my hip bones on the tangle of sharp corners that make up the second floor, but I stay locked in this epic, endless nightmare.

I begin to beg for help, my voice fractured and desperate, but the thunder and scratching sound drown out my cries.

My toes catch on the steps leading up to the third floor. *No, no, no, no.* I need to get to the first floor. I need to run out of the house entirely.

"LAYLA!"

His voice merges into something deadly and unfamiliar as I practically crawl up the stairs, unable to see past my hands as I grope in the dark. I reach the third floor landing as lightning erupts, sending shards of light through the window at the very top of the stairs. I take one look behind me, and my heart nearly leaps out of my chest.

He's standing at the bottom of the stairs. His eyes glow in the darkness, narrowed and cat-like. Not Dalton. This isn't Dalton. It was never, ever Dalton.

My scream shatters all around me but cuts off abruptly when someone's hand clasps around my upper arm and yanks me from the top of the stairs. I'm pulled through a doorway. The door slams shut, and then all of the sudden, the voices stop, and the scratching ceases, and the only sound is me choking on my own breath.

Dalton steps into view. I jerk away, my lips parted as a scream wrenches up my throat, but he clasps a hand over my mouth and presses me to the wall.

"Quiet," he says in a dry, commanding tone. My heart races as he keeps me pinned against the wall. His warmth seeps into my skin, thawing the icy numbness clouding my senses. Outside the door, footsteps travel back and forth, followed by that scurrying, scratching sound.

Then the footsteps are gone, just like that.

I meet Dalton's eyes, tears still sliding from my lashes.

He slowly takes his hand from my mouth, caressing my face instead, his eyes bright and full of concern. An oil lantern illuminates the snug room behind him, a bed and dresser coming into view.

"Is this real?" I manage to say, fighting past a sob.

In answer, he leans in, resting his forehead against mine as his lips gently brush over my own. I feel his touch—warm and rough, just like earlier in the day when he'd found me at the cemetery.

"This is real," he rasps, and presses his lips to mine. "Layla, this is real."

15

LAYLA

I WRAP my hand around the back of Dalton's neck, my nails raking over his skin. His hair is like silk–soft and thick–and his skin is warm against my touch.

He's here; he's real, and I'm safe.

His lips brush against mine again in a silent invitation. My heart is still hammering in my chest as I close my eyes and part my lips, letting go of the crushing weight of the fear I'd just experienced and everything I thought I'd seen while running for my life through the house.

His tongue slides over my lower lip–tasting me. I inhale a desperate breath before his tongue slides into my mouth, over my teeth, my tongue.

He makes a low, throaty sound of pure male satisfaction before pressing his hand against my throat and deepening the kiss until I'm gasping for air.

He tastes like salt and scotch. His leather and spice scent coils around me as he holds me against the wall, his tongue lapping around mine before he lowers his kisses to my jaw, then that sensitive place just behind my ear that makes me melt into a puddle of desire.

My nipples harden and peak beneath my soft linen pajama shirt as he trails kiss after kiss down my neck and back up again. I run my fingers through his hair, pleasantly aware of the sharp citrus scent of the shampoo he uses.

Everything about this moment is tangible. His scent, his touch, his warmth. It's real. He lets go of my throat and clutches my hips, pinning me to the wall as he grinds his hips into mine. I let out a hushed whimper as his rigid cock presses against my sex, only the fabric of my pajamas and his gray joggers keeping us apart.

But my heart is still racing. The memory of being chased through the house by a ghost still sits at the forefront of my mind. That fear turns into something new, mingling with the need throbbing through my body.

"Dalton," I whisper, clutching his shirt. "Am I dreaming?"

His lips dust over my cheek. "No," he rasps, and kisses me again with more urgency. He rests an elbow against the wall beside my head, his other hand embracing my cheek, locking me in place as while his tongue dances over mine.

It's just a kiss. That's all this is. Whatever he's doing is grounding me back to reality, however, and as his touch becomes more heated, I find it harder and harder to pull away and put an end to this.

He's laid waste to my body in my dreams. He's fucked me hard and left me on the edge of release time and time again, and I've always woken up coated in sweat and wholly unsatisfied.

I know that if we take this any farther, I'll give in. I'll submit. I'll do whatever I can to get my next fix. I'll come crawling to him, begging, because no one has ever set my blood on fire in the way he can with just a look in my direction.

With each thrust and swirl of his tongue, the icy hold that memory of the ghost has on my mind gives way, leaving nothing but fevered lust.

He backs away from the wall, taking me with him, his mouth crushed to mine as he spins me around and shoves me onto his bed.

I get my first real glimpse of his room now from flashes of lightning. The raw shiplap walls and plain furniture are nothing fancy. It's a far cry from the haughty, luxurious bedrooms just a level below. Sketches of plants are pinned to the wall near the single window where the storm still rages outside.

I tear my eyes back to his face. He pulls his shirt over his head, revealing his broad, muscular chest littered with tattoos that snake down to his waist. My lips part in surprise as he reaches for the button of his jeans, his chest heaving with a heavy, drawn out breath. His eyes light on mine, a deep emerald in the muted amber light from the oil lantern flickering on the dresser on the far side of the bed. He stands there staring at me, his gaze locked on mine for what feels like eternity as he debates his next move.

Some of that heat slips through my fingertips, replaced by that creeping, icy sensation that I'm being watched, that every darkened corner in this room, and in this house, has a pair of eyes peering at us through the shadows.

My brow furrows as I look up at him from where I lie prone on his bed. He runs his tongue along the inside of his lower lip, looking markedly conflicted about something. I begin to wonder if he's having second thoughts, and now I'm having them. I start to sit up, but his hand juts out and presses me back down on the bed so fast I let out a sharp yelp of surprise.

"Do not move," he tells me in a low, rasping voice. He lets out his breath as he bunches up my shirt, revealing my midriff, then takes my shirt in either hand and twists, ripping the fabric. I suck in a surprised breath, which causes a cocky smile to touch his lips while his eyes gleam with mischief.

"Are you a good girl, Layla?" he says as he slowly begins to tear my shirt down the center. Each thread of fabric gives way in an agonizingly slow fashion that has my heart quickening with each passing second.

"I am," I tell him, breathless. He only smiles down at me and shakes his head.

"You haven't proved that to me yet." He tears the shirt away from my body, baring my breasts. Roughly, he gropes them, kneading them until my nipples harden and peak beneath his touch. My lashes flutter as his touch sends prickles of desires licking over my skin. My need to be touched is at an all-time high, and I rub my thighs together, writhing, trying to create that friction I so desperately need.

"Look at you," he whispers, flicking his thumb over my right nipple. I jerk in response, inhaling sharply at the faint sting. "You're a fucking masterpiece."

I don't dare close my eyes as his heated gaze rakes over my body. He's going to take his time, that's clear. Every touch is deliberate, calculated, like he knows exactly what he wants to do to me and has been thinking about it for a while.

I'm at his mercy.

There's nowhere else I'd rather be.

"Oh!" I cry out, arching my back as his mouth closes around my breast, and he sucks deep, his teeth raking over my nipple. His tongue swirls, lapping at my tender, aching skin. I curl my nails into his backs, scraping hard as he draws a moan from my lips.

But just as I'm giving in to him, to his touch, to the wrongness of this situation, he pulls away with his hand pressed to my throat, pushing me into the mattress.

"Look at me, Angel," he says, his tone dripping with warning.

I clutch his wrist, sucking in a desperate breath. "You're hurting me–"

"Good. This is a punishment." He lets go of my throat and pulls me toward the edge of the bed, his thumbs hooking under my waistband and pulling my pants and panties off in one fluid motion. He tosses my clothes across the room and stands between my knees as he unzips his jeans and pushes them down over his thighs, taking his boxers with them.

My breath catches in my throat at the sight of him naked before me. He's a masterpiece, like his body has been sculpted by a master's hands. Each sharp curve of muscle is dusted with lantern light as he fists his cock. God, *his cock*. I've never seen anything like it. I immediately know this is going to hurt in the best way, but apprehension begins to curl in my stomach as he edges toward the bed, stroking his dick with his eyes locked on mine.

"I warned you not to wander around the house at night, just like I warned you about roaming in the marsh alone."

My reply is a shudder of breath as he pulls me closer to him until my legs fall over the side of the bed. He kneels between my knees, running his hands up my thighs.

"And yet," he rasps as he leans down, brushing the words over my belly, "you continue not to listen to a word I say."

He presses a kiss just below my navel. My core begins to ache as he drags the kiss down, teasingly close to my center, but then he rests his chin on my belly and looks up at me, his eyes dark with what I can describe as cruel intent.

"You haven't been good, Angel."

My lips part, and a choked whimper escapes my throat as his hands yank my thighs apart. I'm fully exposed to him now, my inner thighs wet and glistening. His fingers graze over my sensitive skin, trailing through the glimmers of arousal illuminated by the amber light fanning over our bodies.

He trails a finger through my slit, chuckling darkly. "You're so beautiful, Angel." He kisses the juncture of my thighs.

I close my eyes, gripping the sheets when what I really want to do is grip his hair and press him down to where his mouth would meet my clit.

He chuckles again, grazing his teeth over my inner thigh. "Poor thing," he whispers, his tongue darting out.

I let out a stifled moan and arch my hips to meet his mouth. "P-please—"

"Please what, Angel?"

"Fuck me," I breathe, opening my eyes to find him watching me with interest. "Please, Dalton."

He grazes my inner thigh with his teeth again, "You haven't earned it yet."

"But—why?" Desperation clouds my mind as I writhe against his teasing ministrations.

He bites down on my thigh and I yelp in pain. I try to squirm away, but he bites harder, which blurs the line between pain and pleasure. His fingers are inside of me, sliding into my pussy and stretching me. I nearly arch off the bed when his thumb begins to slowly circle my clit, drawing out a breathy moan from my lips.

He lets up from the bite I know will leave a bruise and rises slightly, his lips parted in a groan as my muscles clamp around his fingers.

"I could make you come right now," he whispers, then blows over my clit. My skin prickles as a chill races up my spine and fans out through my body. "Do you deserve it, Angel?"

I clutch my breasts as he slowly pulls his fingers out and presses them in again with more force, groaning with male satisfaction.

"Please," I beg as he lowers his mouth, his lips hovering over my clit. "I'll do anything."

"Anything?" he laughs, and his the sound skirts over my swollen clit.

I nod, whimpering as he slowly, achingly slowly, pulls out his fingers and drags his tongue up my slit.

My body explodes with pleasure, blurring my senses. I let out a cry and arch into his touch as his tongue slips inside of me, and his lips close around my clit and suck.

Fuck, I'm a goner. I'd grovel at this man's feet in an instant if he demanded it of me.

He hums with approval as I whimper and arch against his tongue, the slight vibration making my vision explode with stars.

I want him inside of me. Whether down my throat, or stretching out my pussy, I don't care. All I know is that this isn't enough. And, the more I think about it, the more I realize he knows that, too.

His touch is teasing, meant to draw this out as long as possible. He slides his fingers back inside of me, hooking them, finding that place that makes me buck my hips off the bed and cry out his name to the ceiling.

"You're fucking delicious," he rasps in a deep, throaty tone. He glides his tongue over and around my clit more, sucking again.

I grit my teeth and close my eyes, my climax beginning to coil through my belly and thighs. My muscles squeeze his fingers involuntarily in warning as I reach that edge, but then he pulls away slightly, right before I come.

"No-no–" I whine, reaching for him.

His cocky smile is the last thing I see before he's fisting my hair and dragging me into a seated position. "Open your mouth. Let me see what that sharp tongue of yours can do."

I look up at him, panting, and open my mouth.

His satisfied smile brightens the room, and the look of pure ecstasy in his eyes as he slowly slides his cock into my mouth has me trembling with excitement and longing.

He's huge–much too big for me. My eyes water as he eases toward the back of my throat, his eyes growing heavy with pleasure.

I let out a whimper as my air supply is stolen. "Can you take all of me, Angel?" he rasps, his jaw flexed as he pulls out slightly, then back in again, further this time, forcing his way down my throat.

Tears spring into my eyes, one of them sliding down my cheek as I choke on his cock, gagging as he hits the back of my throat. "That's a good girl." He grunts, his fingers curling into my hair to hold me steady. His other hand kneads my breast as he holds himself there, unmoving, while I fight for breath. More tears slide free, rolling down my face. He lets go of my breast to wipe it away. "God, you're so pretty when you cry."

His praise ignites a fire within me I hadn't known was there. My pussy aches, begging to be touched, as he pulls his cock from my mouth.

I gasp for breath, my jaw muscles straining, but he shoves his cock down my throat again–hard. Hard enough to leave a bruise in the back of my throat.

I cry out around him, and he growls with delight, his eyes narrowing into cat-like slits. He pumps into me once, twice, then pulls out and shoves me to the bed.

My cheeks are wet with tears as I pant and fight for breath, but he leans over me, nudging my legs apart as he sinks down and guides the head of his glorious cock against my entrance. He kisses me softly, almost tenderly, whispering praise over my jaw and neck while he stretches me open.

I shake as he presses in, then out, my muscles curling around the head of his dick. "You're paradise." He groans, sucking in a breath as he presses his chest to mine and grips my ass, thrusting home.

I cry out his name as pain and pleasure meld into one as he claims me, every rigid inch of his massive cock sheathed to the hilt in my pussy.

"Fuck, Layla," he whispers, beginning to grind his hips against mine. "You're fucking tight. You're so good, Angel. Such a good girl…"

My skin glistens with sweat as he glides over me, breathing my name into my ear, telling me how good I am, how good I feel. His praise sets my blood on fire.

I'm going to come any second now. I can feel that delicious tension beginning to fracture and snap.

"Come for me," he demands, pressing a rough kiss to my neck, then my breasts, his teeth grazing my skin.

"Dalton, please!" I cry out, canting my hips to meet him stroke for stroke.

"That's it, Angel," he rasps as my muscles clamp and spasm around his cock, my climax tearing through my body.

He sucks one of my nipples into his mouth, his tongue swirling over it, drawing out every ounce of pleasure he can from my body as he pumps into me so hard. He bites down hard enough to leave a mark, and spills himself inside me while I milk him dry.

He rises, caging me in with his hands pressed to the mattress on either side of my shoulders. His green eyes shine like polished jade as he looks down at me appraisingly. "Who do you belong to?"

"I belong to you," I whisper, breathless, riding a high I'm not sure I'll ever come down from. "I belong to *you*."

16

DALTON

THE POWER IS STILL out an hour later. I lean my weight against the window sill, rain seeping through the screen as I take a drag from my cigarette and look at the wind-beaten marsh beyond the boundary of the backyard. The storm is finally moving away, the dark clouds funneling in the distance as the storm nears the Gulf. What little moonlight there is to be had illuminates the room in pale silver.

Dressed in only my sweatpants, the cool, stormy air brushes over my naked chest as I keep my eyes on the cemetery in the distance.

Hearing Layla's anguished screams for help earlier tonight rocked me to my core, and there's nothing I can do to ease her fear now. No, this has gone too far. This place has already sunk its teeth into her flesh, and there's no escape now--for either of us.

Another drag of my cigarette clears my head enough to break out of the sex-fueled haze I've been languishing in for the last hour, standing by the window while listening to the house rage all around me.

The door rattles for the hundredth time. I pay it no mind.

I turn and lean my back against the wall, crossing my arms as I watch Layla sleep. Her back is to me, her hair falling like sheets of gold across my pillow. My bed will smell like her tonight–that sweet, honeysuckle scent that has me in a chokehold. I'm supposed to be running her out of this house, this town, not watching her sleeping naked and prone in my bed.

She stirs, shifting her position ever so slightly to lie on her side, which causes the sheets to slip down over that full, round ass.

My jaw flexes as I exhale, chewing my bottom lip.

I'm hard again, aching for her. I want nothing more than to feel her clamp down on my cock while she comes. God, that had been paradise.

I'm moving toward the bed before I can stop myself. I climb out of my joggers and slide in beside her, rolling her over onto her stomach. She makes a sleepy little noise of surprise, lifting her head.

"Shhh…" I whisper. I slide on top of her and guide my cock between her legs. She's fucking soaked all right, and it takes little effort to bury my cock inside her tight, wet pussy in a single thrust.

She moans, arching her hips to meet me stroke for stroke as I slowly pull out and press in again, taking my time and relishing in the feel of her clamping down around me. She fits me like a glove. Like she was made for me.

I lean down, tangling my fingers in her hair, and growl into her ear, "Who do you belong to?"

"You," she moans, sucking in a breath as I continue to rail into her from behind. Her fingers curl into the pillow, her brow furrowed in concentrated bliss. "I belong to you–oh, God, Dalton–"

"Good girl," I rasp, already on the edge of release. I guide her hips upward, wrapping my arm around her waist to hold her exactly where I need her. "You're such a good girl."

I feel her climax building with each thrust, her walls tightening around mine in warning. I let out my breath in a groan when she comes undone around me, crying out my name to the ceiling, and I unleash myself, coming hard still buried inside of her.

I clutch her to my chest as we lie in bed together, her lashes brushing over my skin as she fights to stay awake. I barely sleep as it is, but with her lying beside me, I find it practically impossible.

Every thump and bump in the night carries new weight as I brush my knuckles over her arm, my eyes locked on the ceiling. If I stay awake, I can stop her before she falls back into a dream. If I stay awake, I can keep my eyes on the shadows creeping closer to the bed from every corner. But my eyes grow heavy, and the rain stops, the room around us dropping into suffocating silence.

It's nearly morning when I get out of bed and dress, slipping a shirt over Layla's head. I pick her up, still wrapped in a sheet, and carry her out of the room. Her head lulls on my shoulder as she sleeps, unaware that I'm laying her down in her own bed and tucking her in tight. I pull back the curtains, letting in the first rays of sunshine dusting over the property in the promise of heat and mild weather.

The power kicks back on twenty minutes later as I crouch in my studio, stretching a length of canvas over a frame.

Shortly thereafter, I hear the crunch of tires bouncing over the cracked cement in the driveway. I edge away from the table where I'd been mixing paint and stand beside the window, just out of the glare of the sun.

Bailey steps out of her car dressed in pale pink scrubs that bring out the deep cinnamon of her skin. She pushes her dark curls behind her ears as she squints up at the house, a soft smile touching her lips as she exhales deeply and smiles.

She's innocent and oblivious.

I wish Layla had had that kind of freedom from this place.

But once the demon that lives here sinks its talons into a person's flesh, it's over. I would know, because it happened to me, and now I'm trapped just like Layla will be if I don't keep her out of harm's way.

Laying claim to her means nothing if he's already in her head.

I walk back to my work table and pick up my palette of paint, each shade an attempt to capture the ribbons of gold and platinum that haunt my dreams.

A sketch of Layla–naked and looking over her shoulder–fans out before me as I lift my brush to the canvas.

17

LAYLA

MONDAY MORNING HITS me like a ton of bricks. The sun is shining hot and heavy when I roll out of bed at nearly 10:00, blinking rapidly to adjust to the startling glare. I slept like the dead. No dreams fractured my mind last night but...

I sit on the edge of the bed, dressed in a men's shirt that smells like Dalton.

My throat bobs as I swallow against the sudden tightening there. A dull ache spreads up my inner thighs, and a bite mark I know is on my left breast sings with awakening pain.

Memories of last night crawl back to the forefront of my mind while I sit in the hot sun. Last night, a storm of epic proportions rolled over the property, leaving destruction in its wake. I rise from bed and walk to the window, seeing Curtis on the back lawn cleaning up branches and debris.

Deep puddles glisten in the sunlight–and beyond the yard?

The marsh is lost beneath a thick layer of fog, long silver tendrils rolling back from the tree line as the sun cuts through the shadows.

By midday, it'll be stifling, and the lingering darkness will have nowhere to hide.

I close my eyes and lift my face to the sun, letting the warmth spread over my skin. It's daytime. Every corner of the house will be lit. There will be no shadows. No ghosts.

I'm not sure if what happened to me last night was a dream. Being chased around the house by a ghost feels like something I made up, some revival of the deeply rooted fears I've kept buried since I came here and realized the house didn't feel right.

But Dalton... that had been real. The bruises and bite marks on my body are real. The way I can still smell him on skin, taste him on my tongue, and feel his touch is the realest thing I've ever experienced. My fingertips absently trail down my neck as I continue to stare outside, pretending it's still Dalton's touch. I imagine his lips brushing over my cheek, his teeth grazing the top of my ear as he whispers my name and asks me who I belong to.

He made that clear last night. He made it clear with every stroke, every touch, and every whispered word of pure, unadulterated possession.

Something clatters to the ground in the hallway, and I turn toward my door, listening as Bailey curses under her breath and her footsteps quicken, then recede.

It's Monday. A normal day. I have a shift tonight. I'll be too busy to dive any deeper into the pool of madness that has been trying to pull me under lately.

I pull Dalton's shirt over my head, laying it out on the bed, and shower.

Thirty minutes later I'm downstairs in the kitchen. Bailey leans against the counter, a smile beaming on her face as she recounts her glorious weekend in New Orleans. Sitting at the kitchen table, I sip a cup of coffee and listen to her sing-song voice, my skin warmed by the sun filling the pale green room with the kind of light needed to keep the shadows at bay.

But through the gloomy haze just beyond the archway leading

into the dining room, I swear I see someone sitting at the table, their graceful hands tapping silently on the mahogany surface.

A blink, and the image is gone.

"Did you hear me?" Bailey teases, rolling her eyes as she cuts the turkey sandwich she's been making for the last few minutes in half.

"Oh, I'm sorry," I murmur, swallowing past the lump in my throat. "What did you say?"

"I asked if you want half of this."

"Sure." I give her my best smile as she hands me the sandwich. She begins to sit across from me when her watch beeps. Sighing, she stares down at the tablet propped against the coffee machine.

"Shoot, I better go check on that." She looks down at her uneaten sandwich with a sigh.

"What's going on?"

"Ms. Penny started a new medication this weekend under Vera's direction. I'm not so sure about it. Her stats have been…. Well, here." She hands me the tablet, which glows with the readings of Penny's ECG. Her heart rate is surprisingly low. Notes on the side of the screen show her medication list and dosing chart.

"Why is she taking amobarbital?" I ask, looking up at Bailey with a markedly concerned expression.

"I don't know." Bailey's voice is steady, but serious, and the glint behind her eyes shows me she's just as concerned as I am. "I've been trying to make sense of it since I got here this morning. Vera was halfway out the door when I showed up, barely giving me a rundown of her stats from the weekend."

I stand, pressing my hands to the table. "Penny has dementia. Why is she being treated for… psychosis? I've never seen anyone prescribed amobarbital outside of a psychiatric setting." My mind reels. None of this feels right.

"I have the same question. I've been questioning her prescriptions since I started working here a year ago." Bailey's voice drops to a tone I've never heard from her before. It's almost like she's been wearing a mask of eternal sunshine the entire time, and now the mask has slipped. "She's not deep enough in the throes of late stage dementia to require full sedation like this. Even so, this course would be highly inappropriate regardless of her mental state. She's not a danger to herself or anyone around her, but she's being treated as such. That's what we're doing, Layla, keeping this poor woman fully sedated."

"But… no. This doesn't make any sense–"

"She needs sunshine and socialization. Real food and activities." Bailey runs her hands over her face. "I've been fighting for changes for a while now, and Vera gets in my way every time!"

"Vera?"

"Yes!" Bailey throws her hands in the air. "She's been here for decades. Since she was our age. She's the one who gets to talk to the doctor. She's in control of everything."

Vera's sharp insistence that I leave her, and Aunt Penny, alone all weekend creeps back through my memories. "What the hell is going on?"

Bailey turns her expression to steel and shakes her head. "I don't know, but this medication isn't appropriate at all. Her doctor is coming today. I plan to talk to him about it directly. This should never have been prescribed, nor the blood pressure medication, nor any of the other obscure antidepressants." Bailey sets her untouched sandwich down and tucks the tablet under her arm. "This is wrong."

"I agree," I tell her, reaching out to gently clutch her forearm in solidarity. "I have your back. I have connections all over. We can find her a new doctor."

She nods, a grateful look in her eyes. "I'll speak to her doctor first and see what can be done. I need to go check on her, though."

I release my grip on her arm, and she walks away, leaving me alone and reeling in the kitchen.

My heart skips a beat as I sink into one of the chairs, resting my face in my hands.

I'm not sure how long I sit there letting my mind tangle over Aunt Penny's situation. I hear the front door slam shut, the sound echoing down the snug hallway leading off the kitchen.

A deep, male voice sounds throughout the lower level of the house. "Hello?"

I walk to the foyer. This must be the doctor keeping my aunt in a state of inky, dark submission.

"Hello," I say calmly, politely. "How can I help you?"

The man, an older gentleman in his sixties, with thick glasses and a burly build, looks me up and down. "I'm Dr. Ashford. And who are you?"

"Layla Bryant. The night nurse."

"Ah," he says, his wide mouth ticking into a smile.

"Nurse Bailey is upstairs with my aunt." I eye him skeptically. "Do you know the way, or would you like me to escort you?"

He picks up on my clipped tone of voice and raises his wiry brows. "I know the way."

I step out of his way as he crosses over to the staircase, casting me another appraising glance before walking with heavy tread up the stairs, disappearing from sight.

I spend the next hour going through each bottle of medication in the supply room, counting out the doses, trying to make sense of the gravity of the situation. How long has Aunt Penny been kept under a blanket of sedation like this? Months? Years? Why did it not occur to me before that this was a problem?

It might have been decades.

My stomach curls in on itself as I sit at the janky computer near the window where we're supposed to keep our shift notes. I look back through the notes as far as they go and notice how little is written down whenever Vera has a shift. In fact, before Bailey came, there's barely any records available.

A sharp screech erupts from the living room across the foyer from the supply room, sending a ripple of noise through the air. St. James Infirmary begins to play, skipping every few chords. *"I'm-I'm-I'm goin' down to St-St-St-James In-In-In-"*

I pop out of the computer chair and haul ass to the living room, my heart in my throat. I swear I put the record away. I'm about to take it off the gramophone when Dr. Ashford's voice booms from behind me, "A fan of Cab Calloway?"

I take the needle off the record. "No, actually."

"Well, you're missing out. He's a legend in jazz." Dr. Ashford steps to my side, peering over my shoulder at the record. "Oh, wow. An original record. This is older than I am."

His dangerous close proximity is entirely unnerving as he reaches over my shoulder, slowly pressing the needle back down. "We should listen to it."

"No, I have a lot to do before my shift–"

His hand presses against my lower back. "Turn it back on."

My fight or flight senses kick in, my nerves going haywire. He's at least four times my size. I can feel inhumane strength in his demanding touch as he begins to press me into the table where the gramophone rests. It doesn't make any sense. He shouldn't be this strong. He's so old, and yet the force of his touch is enough to make me cry out in pain as he continues to push me down until I'm pinned.

"Get off–" I squeak, the edge of the table biting into my hip bones.

His other hand snaps to my neck, squeezing so hard my vision begins to go blurry. I choke, grabbing at his wrists and digging my nails into his skin until I draw blood. I can't find the breath I need to scream when he leans over me, his tongue darting out and sweeping over the back of my neck.

"I can taste your fear."

I rake my nails over his wrist, my heart leaping in desperation as my lungs scream for the oxygen he's depriving me of. He wrenches my head to the side, crushing his lips to mine. His tongue jabs into my mouth, down my throat.

A silent scream rips from my body.

I bite down on his tongue, and he wrenches away, stumbling backward. His blood fills my mouth–acrid and disgusting–as my body crashes into the gramophone table. The record kicks back on, the song blasting through the room.

"You fucking bitch," he growls, raising a meaty hand in my direction. Just as he begins to swing, his aim aligned with my face, the window behind us shatters, spraying glass all over my back, and hair. Something black whizzes through the air before falling in a heap in the center of the room.

I fall to my knees as Dr. Ashford staggers backward, his dark, beady eyes clouding with confusion and surprise. I clutch my bruised throat as I look up at the man. He takes one look at me and darts out of the room, tearing through the front door and out of sight.

My body begins to tremble as I kneel in a shower of glass.

I hear it crunching on the far side of the room and look up to find Dalton standing in the archway leading out of the dining room, his face a mask of concern. His lips part like he's about to say something, but a door on the second floor slams shut, and then light footsteps are moving rapidly down the stairs.

"Stay here. Bailey is coming," Dalton says hurriedly, and scoops up a dead crow, its blood soaking into his shirt as he turns with the bird and disappears into the shadows of the dining room once again.

I turn my gaze to the shattered window, its sharp edges coated in blood and black feathers.

Bailey skids to a stop in front of me, looking around wildly.

"Oh, my God, Layla! Are you all right?!"

18

LAYLA

BAILEY PULLS ME UPRIGHT. My legs shake as she guides me to a dusty couch and sits me down, her hands on either side of my face. "God, you're covered in glass–"

"I'm fine," I choke out, but tears sting my eyes as she lovingly reaches up to pick shards of glass from my hair, collecting them in her open palm.

"What happened?"

"A–a bird–" I swallow the words, my throat burning over each syllable. My throat aches and my skin burns where the doctor licked my neck.

Bile rises in my throat at the memory, heightened by the taste of his blood lingering in my mouth. I press my hands to my lips, gagging. Bailey starts, looking wildly around for something for me to throw up in before gripping me hard and dragging me to the small half-bathroom just off the foyer where I throw up in the toilet.

A few minutes later, I'm sitting at the kitchen table while Bailey industrially picks the remaining glass from my hair and tends to several lacerations to my arms I hadn't noticed until the throes of nausea cleared, and my wounds began to burn. "I'm okay," I tell her.

"I'll have Curtis look for the bird. I didn't see it in the living room so it must be flying around the house somewhere. He'll need to replace that window anyway."

I start to tell her Dalton already took care of the bird, but instead suck in my breath and wince at the burn from the alcohol as she dabs my skin. Her eyes meet mine, a sympathetic smile touching her lips, but then her gaze drops to my neck and flashes with concern. "Layla…"

"It's nothing. I must have–I must have done it myself." My words fall flat, but I haven't processed what happened with the doctor yet. I can't find the words to tell her what happened to me.

"I'm going to call the doctor back here, he just left so he can't be far–"

"No!" I grab her hands. "No–I'm fine, really."

She sucks in a breath and shakes her head. "You don't look fine."

"It just scared me, that's all." I swallow past the roiling in my chest, finding it hard to catch my breath as the lie falls from my lips. I don't know why it's so hard to tell her what happened. Everything just… happened so fast.

"Look, I can stay late tonight if you need the night off–"

"No, Bailey, it's all right." I blink away my tears and wipe my face, shivering through the chill that snakes down my spine. "I'm just going to go lie down for a while, at least until the end of your shift."

"Okay," she whispers, smiling calmly down at me as she rises and squeezes my shoulder. "I talked to Dr. Ashford about Ms. Penny's medications, and… I think we should try to connect her with a new doctor after all. I'll call her lawyer and see if he can help us make the transition. For the meantime, I'm taking her off the amobarbital and her blood pressure meds. When Vera comes in this coming weekend and throws a fit about it, I'll take the fall."

"We'll have a solution figured out by then," I tell her, smiling. "Thank you for looking out for my aunt like this, Bailey."

"Go get some rest. I'll come check in on you in a little while."

I nod and rise, sniffling a bit as I slowly glide through the house. I head straight to the bathroom in my room where I sink to my ass in the shower and sit in the scalding hot water, letting it spray over me and wash the doctor's touch from my skin.

When I leave the bathroom wrapped in a towel, I'm not alone.

Dalton sits on the edge of my bed, his hands resting on his knees as he stares absently down at his sneakers. When I close the bathroom door behind me, he looks up then rises. His jade eyes sweep over my face, then my neck, and his concerned expression shifts to something dark and absolutely murderous.

"Dalton–"

"What happened?" he asks, his voice low and vengeful.

My breath catches in my throat as he slowly stalks toward me until he's at arm's length. He reaches out, running his thumb over the finger-shaped red bruises on my neck. His upper lip pulls back in a snarl.

"I–I don't know what happened–"

"The doctor did this," he says to himself. "He touched you."

His hand comes around the back of my neck with little force, his thumb resting over my pulse. "Dalton, I'm fine."

He looks like he wants to break something in half. His eyes leave my neck long enough to scan the scratches on my arms before he meets my eyes. His tongue darts out, gliding along his lower lip. "What did I say?"

"What–what do you mean?"

"What did I say to you last night, Angel?"

No one touches you but me. No one touches you and lives to tell the tale.

"Dalton–"

He lets me go, backing away several steps. "Go to bed," he commands, his voice hollow and emotionless, then he storms out of my room and slams the door behind him.

"Dalton!" I race after him, clutching the towel to my chest as I rush into the hallway, but he's gone.

I look around then walk up the stairs to the third floor, hoping he's just gone to his room. His eyes were so full of rage and hatred. I know Dalton to be steady, not a hot-head, but that look in his eyes makes me wonder if this situation caused him to snap.

I reach his room and raise my fist to knock but then think better of it. The last thing I need right now is a fight. My throat throbs as the bruises set in deep. I'm sure they'll be a grisly yellow in a matter of hours. I'm thankful Bailey hadn't said much about it. I'm not sure I could articulate the truth at that moment.

When I return to my room, I lean against the door to close it, sinking down to the floor and letting my legs splay out in front of me.

Sunlight plays over the room, dust hanging in midair.

I don't rise from the floor for another twenty minutes, and when I do, I simply crawl into bed and bury my face in my pillow where my tears flow freely.

I fall asleep sometime in the earlier afternoon and wake to another gray, stormy sky. No rain yet, but I can smell it in the air as I push the sheets down and sit up, running my hands over my face.

A single rose rests on the edge of the bed, its thorns gleaming in the stormy sunlight. Chills waft over my body as I lean forward to pluck it from its resting place. The thorns are wet, but it's not... not water.

I drop the rose and look down at my palm, and the smear of blood left behind.

19

COLD WATER CASCADES from my hands. The water flows down the sink in crimson ribbons.

Out the kitchen window, night has fallen. Lightning flashes in the distance, but tonight's storm passes the house without much drama. Rain showers over the landscaped backyard in gentle sheets of silver illuminated by the porch light.

I shake my wet hands in the sink, reaching for a towel. My brushes are laid out on the counter, all of them clean and glistening in the light coming from a lamp near the kitchen table.

I gather my brushes and turn, the glint of metal catching my eye.

A butcher knife rests in the dish rack, freshly sharpened.

It's the only thing in the dish rack. Both Bailey and Layla keep the kitchen spotless and would have noticed a knife being left out. I reach for it and pull it off the rack just as Layla walks into the kitchen.

Dressed in pale blue scrubs with her hair pulled back, I can see every bruise and scrape on her arms and neck. Her neck is a ghoulish yellow color which makes fury rear its ugly head inside of me again,

125

and her eyes are nearly the same color blue as her scrubs but lined with red from crying. She refuses to look at me as she edges toward the sink, her eyes locked on the butcher knife.

She goes to drop a mug in the otherwise empty sink and stops when she sees the remaining ribbons of dark crimson still swirling toward the drain.

"It's paint," I remark dryly, putting the knife in its proper place—the drawer next to the dishwasher.

"What else would it be?" she asks rhetorically, turning the water back on to rinse her coffee mug. She glances at the clock on the microwave. It's just after 9:00, but the dark circles under her eyes are already visible as she looks between the microwave, coffee maker, and the mug she just deposited in the sink.

"I can make another pot of coffee if you want. I'll be up for a while, too. Could probably use the caffeine."

She glances at me, her throat bobbing as she swallows. "Where have you been all day?"

I roll my brushes in the palm of my hand. "Painting."

"Where?"

"The cigar room."

"I went there earlier to try to talk to you, and you weren't there."

"I might have been in my studio then."

Her eyes lock on mine. I arch my brow and lean my hip against the counter. "Did you want more coffee or not?"

"Did you leave me another rose?"

"No, I did not."

"What kind of game is this, Dalton?"

She looks so exhausted. In fact, her entire body sags as her words fall between us. I watch her for a moment, debating whether or not it's time to tell her the truth, but the less she knows, the better, especially now that she's sleeping again and more clear headed than she's been the past couple of weeks.

"I'm not playing a game," I tell her, keeping my gaze locked on her face. "I didn't leave you a rose. I didn't leave you a rose the first time, either."

"Then who did?"

"Maybe Bailey—"

"No," she breathes, shaking her head.

I roll my lower lip between my teeth and shrug. "Your aunt, perhaps?"

A glimmer of frustration flashes behind her eyes. "That's not funny."

"It's probable, though, isn't it?"

"She's barely lucid."

"That's going to change though, isn't it?" She stares at me, realizing I know a lot more about Penny's situation than I let on. "I want you to stay away from Vera this weekend."

"Why?"

"Isn't it obvious she's up to something when it comes to your aunt?" I set my brushes down on the counter and cross my arms over my chest. "You promised you'd obey me. I'm forbidding you—"

"This is my job, Dalton! You can't forbid me from doing anything, especially not conversing with a fellow nurse."

I kick off the counter and cage her in on the other side of the kitchen, my hands resting on either side of her head against the upper cabinets, the green vinyl surface cool to the touch. "Do I need to remind you who I am and the deal we made last night?"

She sucks in her breath, the artery in her neck fluttering as her pulse quickens.

"Do as I say. Stay away from that woman."

"Tell me why—"

"Do you think your aunt is the only person she fucks with while she's in the house?" I snarl.

She narrows her eyes at me. I push off the cupboard and step away, my eyes still locked on hers. "Are you insinuating that she's drugging me?"

"She could be."

"What reason would she have to do that?"

"What reason does she have to keep your aunt in a stupor?"

Her throat bobs again, highlighting the bruises that make my blood boil. I hold my ground for another moment, waiting for Layla to say something, anything, but she tries to walk past me into the hallway. I grab her arm. "We're not done here."

"I've had a fucking awful day, Dalton," she snaps, wrenching her arm from my grasp.

"The doctor has something coming for him, Layla."

She freezes, glancing up at me. "What are you going to do?"

I turn to face her, resting a hand on the doorway to prevent her from escaping down the hallway. "Nothing," I whisper, leaning to brush the word over her cheek. "Not me."

She sucks in a breath as my lips graze her cheek then that spot below her ear that makes her tremble. She lets her breath out in a shaky moan then snaps her back to her senses, and she shoves me away. Her eyes blaze with heat and anger as she looks up at me. "What do you want from me right now, Dalton?"

"I want you on your knees," I rasp and pull her toward me to kiss her again. "I want to touch you everywhere that vile man dared touch. I want to wash his taste out of your mouth and remind you who you belong to."

She melts into my touch. I cage her against the counter. I continue, "I warned you what would happen if anyone else touched you. I made it clear who you belong to, and that's me. It'll only ever be *me*." I kiss her hard, my tongue sweeping over her lower lip before plunging inside her mouth–tasting, teasing, flicking over her teeth. She arches her neck back, and I trail kisses over each bruise left by the doctor's fingers, my hands roaming under her scrub top until I reach her bra. I squeeze her breasts, loving how full and heavy they are in my hands. "You're mine. *Mine.* I want to hear you say it. I need to know that you understand who you belong to."

She's panting, her eyes pinched closed as I kneel in front of her.

"Say it, Angel," I repeat more firmly then press a kiss to her stomach, my thumbs hooking into her waistband and pulling her pants and panties down to her knees.

My answer is a sharp intake of breath as I drive two fingers into her soaking wet pussy, hooking them to meet that spot I know sends her head spinning. She clutches the edge of the counter, leaning her back against it as her legs tremble.

"Say it," I demand against her clit, my breath brushing over the swollen, sensitive parts of her I'd love to bury my cock into right now, but she hasn't earned it yet.

"I'm yours," she whimpers, throwing her head back.

"That's my good girl." I growl then slide my tongue over her clit and through her folds.

She tastes like paradise, sweet and heady, and hot to the touch. I devour her like I'm starving, each swipe of my tongue and thrust of my fingers making her even wetter. She drips down my fingers onto her panties. I graze my teeth over her clit, and she lets go of the counter and grabs my hair, tangling her fingers in it and pulls.

I growl against her inner thigh. "Easy, Angel."

But she's already on the edge of coming completely undone. I can't have that. I only want her coming on my cock from now on.

I bite her inner thigh and pump my fingers inside her a few more times, loving the way she writhes against my hand, then I'm back on my feet unzipping my jeans. I pull her panties back up–a little black thong. I'd love to bind her wrists together with it while I fuck her from behind, but I don't have time to mess with that now.

I flip her around and press her down against the counter, one hand on her upper back to keep her still, then hold her thong to the side. I nudge her legs apart, which gives me a glimpse of her beautiful, wet pussy. I drag the head of my dick over her entrance once, twice, then slam into her. She jerks, whimpering from the impact. She tries to press her hands against the counter to push herself upright, but I gather her wrists and hold them against the small of her back while pumping into her.

The slapping of our bodies merges with the steady thumps of the rain hitting the porch roof.

"Please, Dalton!" she cries out, her pussy tightening around my cock.

"That's it, Angel." I moan, closing my eyes and losing myself to the way she feels with each thrust. "I know you love it." She's so tight, so unaccustomed to a cock my size, but she takes all of me without a fight. "You're doing so good."

She cries out, her pussy spasming as her climax echoes through her body. I let my head fall back. This is ecstasy, but I pull out at the last second and grab her thong, coming all over her panties.

She looks at me over her shoulder with an arched brow, her skin flushed pink. "Did you just–"

"You'll wear them until I come find you again later tonight."

"Why?"

"To remind you that I am in control, Angel." I let go of her wrists and zip my jeans, watching as she adjusts her panties and pulls up her scrub pants, a fiery blush staining her cheeks.

When she looks up at me again with those doe eyes, I tap the underside of her chin.

"Do not walk around in the dark tonight," I command, my eyes locked on hers. "Or there will be repercussions."

20

LAYLA

I SHOULDN'T LOVE Dalton's dominance and force as much as I do. My ears are still ringing with his praise as I spend the next several hours tending to my aunt. She's sleeping soundly, peacefully. All of her stats are still in the green. I read over Bailey's notes, which she'd written on a notepad instead of typing them into the tablet. When we decided to take her off the two suspicious medications, we'd hatched a plan. We're going to take notes on paper, something we can hide or destroy so it doesn't fall into Vera's hands.

I don't know Vera well enough to say she has a good handle on her pharmaceutical knowledge, but she's been a nurse for decades according to Bailey. I'm under the impression she'll notice we switched out the IV medication for saline and the pills Aunt Penny already struggles to swallow for sugary placebos.

But we have to try. Something must be done.

I watch Aunt Penny sleeping as I tidy up the supplies I used to change out her IV port. Is she still there somewhere, beneath the haze of antipsychotics? Does she have any idea what's going on around her or what's been done to her?

I glance down at my watch. It's just after 3:00 A.M., and the house around me is quiet. My eyes are heavy as I slowly shut her bedroom door and turn toward the stairs with a handful of supplies, then stop, looking down into the beckoning shadows.

Dalton said he'd find me again tonight. My core aches with excitement every time I think about it, but hours have passed since our encounter in the kitchen. He also told me not to wander in the house at night; he demanded that of me, in fact.

I have to discard my sharps downstairs. I'm not going to sit around with a pile of needles all night. There's a difference between wandering and doing my job.

I huff out a breath and look around, half expecting him to jump out of the shadows the second my foot hits the top step, but I'm met with silence.

The house is calm tonight. The storm passed us by miles, leaving nothing but a steady rain in its wake. There's no thunder or lightning shattering the sky tonight. Just rain, and silence, and a calm energy that puts me at ease as I descend the stairs.

I turn on the light to the supply room and discard the sharps. I pull the computer chair over to the plastic table in the center of the room and take my notes from the evening. There's nothing to report to Bailey at this point. It's our first day weening Penny off her useless medications, anyway.

Like we'd agreed earlier in the day, I slip the notepad under a specific box of bandages on the very bottom shelf and turn out the light, walking into the foyer with the intention of getting a few hours of sleep, but a figure moves in the living room.

Cast in shadow, I can't see Dalton's face, but I know it's him based on his build. Unlike the night with the storm, I'm not afraid. That had been a delusion I'd made up in my mind because of the storm. This is real.

He moves to the gramophone on the far side of the room, and

through the faint porch light drifting through the window, I catch his hand pressing the needle down on the record.

"I hate this song," I say, my voice echoing through the empty shadows between us. "St. James Infirmary" scratches to a start, the jazzy chords choking the room.

"I don't care," Dalton whispers, his voice void of emotion.

I swallow, his cold tone making me slightly uneasy. I've noticed that Dalton doesn't hide his anger or frustration. If he's upset with me, it's clear.

This ice in his voice is new.

I've really pissed him off, I guess, having gone against his direct orders and came downstairs at night.

"I know you told me not to wander around the house, but I needed to dispose of the sharps. I know it seems... trivial to you, but imagine—imagine being told you can't wash your paintbrushes off when you're done with them, Dalton. You put me in an impossible situation."

"Come here," he says sternly.

I bristle at his tone and take three steps into the living room.

"Closer."

I shake my head, and his rough laugh echoes over the music.

I move to the side, resting my hand on top of the jet-black grand piano toward the entrance of the room, the surface cool to the touch. I'm tired, not thinking straight.

He slowly moves in on me, each step totally silent. It sends a shiver up my spine, especially as he crosses a beam of porch light drifting through the curtains that does nothing to light up his face.

I step back in sudden fear, my heart beats quickening.

He chuckles low, the sound rising over the music as he comes to stop only two feet away from me. "Are you afraid of me, Layla?"

"Sometimes."

"Hmm...." He edges closer, leaning down and reaching out to tap one of the piano keys. The chord rings through the air over the song. "You're unique, Layla. Your fear lights a fire within you, but not one meant for survival. No... for you, it begs you to submit, doesn't it?"

My throat tightens when he grazes his knuckles over my arm.

"It's why you didn't fight back against the doctor, isn't it?"

I try to pull away from him, but he grabs my throat. I freeze.

"I don't like this," I rush out. "I don't want to play–"

"I wasn't asking." He growls, and then he's pressing me against the side of the piano, leaning over me. He doesn't kiss me, but he continues to squeeze my throat until I gasp. Through the hazy shadows covering his face, all I can see is the glint of his teeth as he smiles wickedly at me.

He reaches for me, roughly shoving one of his hands down my pants, and strokes my center. Grinning madly, he pulls his hand out and lifts it up to the shreds of light hanging in the air. My wetness gleams on his fingers. "I was right."

I barely have a second to catch my breath before he's pulling my pants down.

I should stop him. I should say something now that he's pushing me against the piano and lifting me up. I wrap my legs around his waist as the smooth piano cools my back. I'm not sure I like this. I should say no, I should say the way his fingers tangle in my hair hurts, but I don't. I shouldn't feel like this--I shouldn't love this thrill of being hunted and chased through the dark and taken by force, but I do, and I trust him not to hurt me.

But when he climbs on top of me and thrusts his massive cock inside of me, it hurts. I try to pull away, but he clutches me tighter, his fingers digging into my waist. "Is this what you want, Layla?" He grunts, pushing all of his weight into me. I choke out a moan, my legs already trembling.

"You're a filthy slut," he rasps in my ear. "The way you grip my cock–God–" He groans, planting one hand on the top of the piano as he slams into me again and again.

This is punishment. I've been bad. I didn't listen to him.

"Come for me," he commands through gritted teeth.

"I–I–" I'm not there yet. I can feel it building but... I need more.

He grabs my throat, squeezing hard enough to steal my breath. "Come. For. Me."

I feel myself slipping into unconsciousness, my lungs screaming for air. "D-Dalton–I can't breathe–"

He has me pinned beneath him. I can't move. I'm losing my grip on reality as the muscles in my legs strain with each of his thrusts. Despite it all, my building climax explodes, that tension that'd been pooling in my core for hours now giving way and flooding my body with tidal waves of pleasure.

He chuckles right in my ear as he pulls out, yanking me off the back of the piano with him. I land on my knees yelping with pain.

"You didn't deserve that, you whore. The next time I catch you with another man, you'll pay for it with more than your cunt."

Shock ripples through me, my fingertips prickling with adrenaline as my chest tightens around his words. I've never heard him like this. His fury penetrates the very air I'm desperately trying to gulp down as he rises above me and simply walks away, disappearing into the shadows of the dining room.

It takes several minutes to find my bearings. Shaking, I pull my pants up, my heart heavy with shame and confusion. I stumble to the couch and sit down, wincing at the pain between my thighs.

Tears begin to slide down my cheeks as I lie down on my side, tucking my hands between my legs.

The house falls into total silence. The rain tapers off. The storm clouds part, and right before I fall asleep, I catch a glimpse of the stars.

When I wake, I'm back in my own bed. It's too early for the sun to be up, and my room is cast in shadow brought on by my bedside lamp, which is on. How did I get here?

I sit up, blinking into the shadows.

My alarm goes off. It's 6:00 A.M.. Time for Aunt Penny's medications.

I change into fresh scrubs. My inner thighs are bruised, and my throat aches. My eyes are puffy from crying as I glance at my reflection in the mirror for a split second before looking away in shame.

I thought I loved Dalton's dominance, but he's never degraded me before. He's never made me feel worthless.

It hurts more than I'd like to admit.

I walk out into the hallway and turn to shut my door when footsteps sound in the stairwell leading to the third floor.

Dalton comes into view, his eyes bright and... pleased to see me. He even gives me a soft, cocky smile as he passes me in the hallway, turning to look at me over his shoulder while resting his hand on the banister leading down to the first floor. "Thank you," he says.

"For what?" I say, my words wobbling as I refuse to meet his eyes.

"For not wandering around last night. I'm not trying to be mean or–I understand you're a nurse, and your supplies are downstairs–"

I meet his eyes, my body going numb. "What are you talking about?"

"I came to find you last night and you were already asleep. I wanted to apologize for what I said in the kitchen. I just don't want you.... This house is dangerous at night, Layla. You know what I'm talking about now." He pauses, shaking his head. "I didn't want to wake you up, but I am sorry."

My stomach bottoms out. "But we–we talked in the living room last night. We–"

The look on his face cuts me to my core. His eyes darken, and his jaw flexes. "I wasn't in the living room last night. I went to my room shortly after I left you in the kitchen." His eyes flare with sudden concern and then a kind of rage I've never seen from him before, but it's not directed at me. He takes a step toward me, his voice dropping an octave. "What's happened, Layla?"

"I can't–" I shake my head, my senses going haywire. He reaches for me, but I brush past him, walking swiftly to my aunt's door.

"Layla!"

I close myself into my aunt's room and lean on the door, fighting for breath. Tears sting my eyes. I try to blink them away, focusing on the ceiling.

Dalton exhales sharply and curses under his breath before his footsteps sound out in the hallway. He stops in front of the door, and for a moment, I imagine him clenching and unclenching his fists before his footsteps start up again and recede out of earshot.

I can't make sense of what happened last night. He'd been there. He'd talked to me, then pressed me to the piano and fucked me with no feeling whatsoever. He'd called me names, told me I deserved the pain he inflicted, and then left me there on the floor.

And now?

Now I'm wondering if I dreamt it up, that I let my mind slip back into that dark place I was in only a few nights ago during the storm.

I take a few moments to center myself.

Then I turn to my aunt whose eyes are open and fixed on the window.

21

I COAT my brush in paint and dab it gently against the wall in the cigar room. With each stroke, the wallpaper is coming back to life. Sunlight drifts through the windows, highlighting the dust my movements disturb with each flick of my wrist.

It's nearly 2:00 in the afternoon. I've been fighting the urge to storm into Layla's room and wake her up, demanding answers.

Something happened to her last night. The look on her face and hurt behind her eyes sets my soul on fire every time I think about our encounter in the hallway early this morning.

Something happened, and whoever did it… they made her think it was *me*.

I clutch the brush so tightly it snaps.

"Fuck." I growl, tossing the pieces onto the plastic at my feet. I rest my hand against the wall, then press my forehead to it, closing my eyes for a moment. "You fucking bastard," I whisper to the room. "I told you to leave her alone. We made a deal."

I'm met with silence, like usual.

Frustrated, and unable to focus, I leave the cigar room. I turn the corner on the second floor that leads to the main hallway and pause, my hand on the railing of the stairs leading up to the third floor. Voices drift up from the first level of the house–The Wilsons. And, to my surprise, Layla. She's not asleep after all.

"Stop it, Robert. You're going to scare her!"

"I want to know!" Layla pleads.

I edge down the hallway, my footsteps practically silent on the floorboards, and press myself against the wall closest to the stairs leading down to the foyer.

"It's common knowledge, Helen. Hell, the historical society has been pushing that lawyer to let them put a plaque on the front gate for some years now."

"A plaque for what?" Layla exclaims, her voice lifted in a laugh.

"The victims of a murderer, which are said to have been lingering here on this property for quite some time." Helen breathes, annoyance lacing every word, "Which, I might add, is not true. The plaque part, at least."

"A murder?" Layla gasps, but it's exaggerated, like she isn't surprised in the slightest.

"Apparently. No one has been able to prove it." Robert chuckles, sighing deeply.

Layla cuts in. "Curtis already told me about the family deaths and fires. He didn't say anything about a serial killer!"

"See, Robert? This is why I told you to keep your mouth shut."

"It's just rumors, darlin'," Robert says to Layla. "But… I'll tell you, if you really want to know."

Helen groans, mentioning something about going out back to talk to Curtis.

"I *do* want to know."

"Well, I'll tell you over a plate of that lemon Bundt cake Helen brought."

Layla's voice retreats as she agrees.

They must be walking into the kitchen. I glance over my shoulder at the doors stretching down the hallway then carefully walk down the stairs, avoiding spots I know will creak if I step down too hard.

"I'll tell you, Miss Layla, that this isn't a serial killer by any means, first and foremost. Secondly, this is all part of the rumor mill, so don't buy any stock in what I'm about to say."

"Based on what Curtis told me, Hahnville has a very active rumor mill," Layla replies over the sound of clattering dishes. "Do you want a big piece or a small piece?"

"Look at me, darlin'. Do you think I've ever asked for a small piece of anything in my life?"

Layla's laugh is like music that settles in my soul. I don't think I've ever heard her laugh so carefree before.

I stand at the bottom of the stairs acutely aware of every sound—of Robert and Layla in the kitchen, of Bailey upstairs in Penny's bedroom. The last thing I need is for Layla to catch me eavesdropping. I'm also aware of a shadow where it shouldn't be in the formal living room to my right. I slowly turn my head toward the darkness, the corner of my mouth ticking into a sly smile.

"There was a strange death in Hahnville some thirty years ago now, back in the early nineties. A young man was found dead about a mile west of here, on the outskirts of the Gregory property." Robert exhales, then continues, "Poor kid was shot six times in the head."

"I imagine there wasn't much left of his head if that's true."

"You're right about that. Took ages to identify the man from what I remember. Around that same time, a woman showed up at a Greyhound station in New Orleans having a psychotic break of some kind. She ended up at an institution in Shreveport. Her name was Milly Appleborough."

"We're the two connected in some way?"

"Oh yes, but nobody knew for a long while. There was a second body found roughly eight years later—another man, but this time it was an officer in our local police force. He went missing for a year before they found his body half buried near the highway leading out of town. Awful mess, that one. The whole town was in a fit over it. Brutal killing, and his young wife ended up being the one who did it."

"What?"

Robert clears his throat. I slowly sink down and sit on the steps, listening intently. "You heard me correctly, miss. His wife killed him, but she didn't do any time, not in prison at least. She was insane, Layla. Lost her mind entirely. When she went down for her husband's murder, they searched their house in town and found the bodies of her father and her brother buried in the crawlspace. They had her locked up at an institution up north, on the East Coast. She died there a few years ago."

Layla's sharp intake of breath echoes down the hallway between the foyer and kitchen. "That's awful, but what does it have to do with *this* house?"

A creaking sound drifts down the hallway, likely from Robert shifting his weight in his chair. "The officer's wife worked here for a few months before the murders. As did Miss Appleborough."

"Were they nurses?"

"No. Miss Appleborough was a drifter, according to rumor. She came to town looking for work and ended up working here as a maid. The man who was shot in the face six times was a chef. He worked in the kitchen during the time when Ms. Penny was still somewhat with us. Miss Appleborough never admitted to the murder, but she couldn't, really. She was in rough shape by the time the police were able to identify the man. Hadn't said more than a few words since the police picked her up in New Orleans, and when she did talk, she rattled on about a demon living in the house and possessing the people inside of it."

Layla says nothing, but I can imagine the look on her face right now.

Robert continues, "The officer's wife, Shelby Morsgate, was said to be having an affair with someone living at this house before her killing spree. She came over and did the laundry every week, a volunteer thing for the church. Ms. Penny was pretty far gone by that point, in the early 2000s, and had a long line of nurses and doctors who worked here, as well as some that occasionally lived here, even for short periods of time. It's rumored Shelby had an affair with one of Ms. Penny's doctors, but nothing was ever confirmed."

"So both women were connected to the house in some way, and they both killed their lovers--or husband?"

"Yes."

My fingers curl over the edge of the step I'm still plastered to, unable to move if I wanted to. I've heard enough but can't tear myself away without hearing Layla's full reaction to the tales Robert spins for her over slices of lemon cake.

"And both women lost their minds?"

"Yes," Robert says, matter-of-factly.

I glance back at the shadow, which seems to be getting closer. "Happy now?" I whisper.

The shadow evaporates like it had just been the result of a cloud passing over the sun, but a chill runs up my spine nonetheless.

I miss the later part of the conversation because of Bailey. I hear the door to Penny's room open, then shut, and I waste no time darting outside to avoid being seen, closing the door quietly behind me.

I walk briskly across the driveway, glancing over my shoulder at the house and grounds. I spot Curtis and Helen talking in the back-yard, but they quickly fade from view as I hurry down the driveway, cutting through a thicket of cypress trees.

It's quiet out here with only the buzzing of insects and chirping of birds for company. The haze of summer beats down on my shoulders as I walk with no clear direction or idea where I'm going or why.

It's not long before the back of my neck begins to prickle, and the forest falls silent.

I turn around, tucking my hands in the pockets of my jeans, and face the one I knew would follow me out here, especially after the conversation that passed between Layla and Robert.

"Nice of you to finally show your face," I say dryly. "It's been a while."

He just stares at me, expressionless. His dark, unblinking eyes hold my gaze as I reach into my back pocket and pull out a cigarette. I bring it to my lips, light it, and then extend the carton to him. "Oh," I chuckle darkly. "I forgot." I tuck the carton back in my pocket and cross my arms. "Can't smoke, seeing as you're… what would you call it?"

The man narrows his eyes, standing unnaturally still.

"Dead?" I ask, my lips curling into a smile around my cigarette. "Or is that not the right term for it, in your case?"

He doesn't move, doesn't so much as take a breath.

"I know what you did," I tell him, exhaling smoke around the words. "I don't appreciate you touching what I claimed as mine. You and I had a deal. She's not part of this. She's off limits. I had your word."

Finally, his mouth flexes into an uncanny smile, like he's not entirely sure how to make the motion. "You never said I couldn't play."

"This isn't a game."

He takes a single step forward. I refuse to retreat, even though every fiber of my being is screaming to run.

"Find someone else to fuck with," I tell him sternly, viciously. "Leave Layla out of this."

"It's too late for that. I've had a taste. She's a Gregory, and they've always been the sweetest."

"And what does Penny think of all of this?" I ask sharply.

Amos's smile fades, his eyes going darker than I thought possible. Penny is a sore spot for this fucker, whatever he is. She was his toy when she was younger, his loyal companion and servant, until she refused to bring him men to torment. Then, she refused to marry and have children, cutting off her family line. All because of him and the torture he'd inflicted on her family for generations.

"That's what I thought," I muse, taking a long drag from the cigarette before flicking it into the brush at my feet, stubbing it out with my shoe. "Let me guess. You have that old bitch Vera doing your bidding? Keep the mistress of the house out cold so you can pray on every person who sets foot through the door without her intervening?"

Amos eyes me coldly. Looking at him gives me a strange feeling, especially since he looks remarkably like me right now. He's trying to, at least. He refuses to answer me, which tells me everything I need to know.

There's one thing I've learned about demons during the time I've had to creep around this godforsaken hell-hole.

They're fucking dumb. Childish, even. Unable to estimate the ripple effect of their actions.

"You've reneged on your end of the bargain. You touched Layla. You *hurt* her, you sick fuck. We're done."

"You'll never be free of me."

"You'll never be strong enough to break me." Like I said, I've lasted way longer than any of the men who've come before me.

The demon and I stare at each other for several long, drawn out moments.

"We'll see." Then, he's gone.

22

LAYLA

BAILEY STIRS sugar into her iced tea, her eyes wide and skeptical. "How many more murders did Robert say were connected to the property?"

"He only said there may have been more, but those two...well, *four*, if you count Shelby Morsgate's family, were the only murders with confirmed connections."

"I've lived in this town my entire life and never knew any of this," she admits, her eyes focusing on the ice clicking in her glass. "Do you think it's true?"

"I don't know what to think." I rest my chin in my hand and stare blankly at the pitcher of iced tea between us, the glass surface frosted and sweating in the unforgiving heat.

Bailey's on break, and I should be asleep, but I doubt I'm going to sleep at all for the next several years after the stories Robert told me.

How is it possible that two women from totally different walks of life ended up following the same path to murder and madness?

"Is it weird I don't find it totally disturbing?" Bailey asks, leaning back in her chair.

"It's because we're nurses." I roll my eyes to the ceiling. "I've seen and heard worse stories."

"Me too," she breathes, wincing a bit. "Still… it makes me wonder about all the noises I hear in the house. Voices, too, sometimes. I never know if what I'm hearing is real."

"Has anyone ever mentioned Aunt Penny going to assisted living? She's gotta have the funds for it."

"I'm sure she does, but no. I've always assumed she lived here because that's what the estate stipulates."

I make a mental note to give Aunt Penny's lawyer a call tomorrow and ask about her executor. Whoever that person is would know exactly why she's here and not someplace where she'd have a far higher level of round the clock care.

Not that Bailey and I aren't capable, but Bailey was right when she said Aunt Penny needs more. More sun. More socialization. Better conditions in general.

She shouldn't be locked away in a rotting house full of ghosts.

"I don't know how you stay here at night alone," Bailey muses, sipping from her tea.

"I'm not alone."

"Ms. Penny doesn't count."

"No, Dalton's here. He's usually awake at night, too."

Bailey blinks at me. "Who?"

"Dalton, the artist who lives upstairs. The guy that's been working on all the wallpaper."

"Did you sneak some whiskey into your tea?" she laughs, waving a hand in dismissal.

"What do you mean?"

"There's nobody else living here, especially not an artist."

"Uh, no… Dalton—"

The tablet between us lights up, then both of our smartwatches begin to blare with an alarm linked to Aunt Penny's ECG machine.

"Shit," I mumble, snatching the tablet and pulling up her stats. I'm on my feet in a split second.

Bailey and I dash up the stairs and into Aunt Penny's room. She's sitting straight up in bed, staring directly ahead, her frail fingers trembling as she grips her sheets.

Bailey edges around the room into her line of sight, her gaze darting between Penny's face and the ECG monitor.

"Her heart rate is extremely high," Bailey says calmly.

"She's stable for now," I answer breathlessly. Penny's not having a heart attack. This isn't an arrhythmia. I see nothing on her monitor that would tell me something is seriously wrong.

This is fear.

"Ms. Penny?" Bailey coaxes, smiling sweetly. "Ms. Penny, honey, you're not feeling well right now, are you? What's the matter?"

Aunt Penny shakes her head, her lips parting.

I move into her line of sight as Bailey closes in on the bed, her hands outstretched. "Ms. Penny, I'm going to help lay you back down now, all right?"

But Aunt Penny's eyes flicker to mine, her expression undergoing a sharp change. Her eyes widen, her slack mouth pinching closed. She shakes her head over and over again.

"Ms. Penny?" Bailey urges, laying a hand on the old woman's thin forearm.

"Run," Penny croaks, her eyes locked on mine.

"What?" Bailey whispers. "What did you say?"

Penny's chest heaves, her eyes wild and frantic. "RUN! Get out! Before–before it's too late! Before he–he finds you. Run! *RUN!*"

I stumble backward, my heart leaping into my throat as she tries to throw her body forward, her arm outstretched toward me.

"Go! Go! Get out! *GET OUT!*"

"Layla, leave," Bailey says firmly, her eyes slightly cloudy.

"I–I—" I gape at Aunt Penny.

"Layla, go. You're agitating her somehow!" Bailey shouts.

I snap out of my stupor and tear myself from the room, shutting the door behind me. I lean against the wall, fighting to catch my breath as I listen to the commotion in the room behind me.

"Who are you? Who are you?"

"I'm Bailey, ma'am, your nurse. Remember?"

"The girl—get her out. He wants her. He'll trap her here. Get her out, please! You have to get her out."

"It's all right now. Just lay back. See? Isn't that better?"

Soon Penny's voice lowers, becoming more calm. Ten minutes pass while I continually check my watch, waiting for what, I'm not entirely sure.

Finally, I hear Penny say, "Do not give me any medication. Don't give me anything. Don't let them give me anything. Please."

"I'm not. I won't—"

"Promise me—"

"Ms. Penny—"

"My-my hands? My hands? Why am I—why am I so old?" Her voice breaks. "What year is it?"

I close my eyes, my heart sinking into my stomach.

"How old am I? How—how old am I?"

If Bailey says anything, it's lost on the quiet whimpering coming from the room.

Ten minutes later, Bailey opens the door, her face washed of color as she slowly closes it behind her.

"She's resting." Tears cloud her eyes. She wipes them away, sniffling. "I gave her lorazepam. It's all she would take. She thought...." She bares her teeth, her eyes pinched shut as if in pain. "She looked at her hands, Layla, and started to cry. She thought she was still young. Still in her *twenties*."

My heart lurches. What happened to this poor woman? It could be the dementia, but maybe not.

Tears spill down Bailey's cheeks, but her eyes narrow, her chest puffing out. "I'm calling her *fucking* doctor right now."

"Bailey—" I start to say, desperation lacing through her name, but she rushes down the stairs. I sigh heavily, running my fingers through my hair and forcing back a sob at not only what just happened, but the idea of Dr. Ashford coming back here.

I stand conflicted in the hallway for a little over two minutes before chasing after her with every intention of telling her the truth about what happened the day that bird flew through the window.

But Bailey is standing in the supply room with her phone pressed to her ear, her brow pinched.

"Okay–okay. Yes. I'm so sorry to hear this, I–I can't really wrap my head around it." She meets my eyes, looking suddenly frantic. "Okay, sure. No, that's not necessary. All right, goodbye." She hangs up and almost drops her phone.

"What's going on?"

"Dr. Ashford is in the hospital. He was–he's in the ICU in really rough shape."

For obvious reasons, this is music to my ears, but I fight the smile threatening to stretch across my lips. "What happened?"

"That was the receptionist at his practice." Bailey sinks into the computer chair, her eyes fixed on the floorboards. "He was attacked. The police are saying it was a burglary. Someone broke into his house and stabbed him several times in his sleep. They don't think he's going to make it."

I take a step backward, my heart racing. "When did this happen?"

"Very early Tuesday morning," she says, running her hand over her face.

I nod because it's all I can do. All I can think about is what Dalton said to me, how Dr. Ashford had something coming his way.

Oh, God. Did he do this?

I feel the urge to vomit but steel my expression. "I guess this solves one of our problems."

Bailey nods. "He was keeping her sedated for God knows how long–or why. Fucking sick, sadistic bastard."

"I'll call around for a new doctor if you can stay tonight to help with Penny."

Bailey nods, her eyes still locked on the floorboards. "I actually know of another doctor who lives here in Hahnville. She works in

New Orleans, but she goes to church with my mom. I'm going to go into town and see if she's home."

"Okay," I say, watching as Bailey rises and walks to the door like a ghost.

She pauses at the door, her fingers curled around the knob. "I think you scared her a little. You look like Penny from her youth, you know. That's all."

I've already let the memory of what Penny said to me in her room slip from my mind. "I know. I think you're right." But not really. There was something else in her warning, something that settles in my bones as Bailey walks out the door and out onto the porch.

I walk back upstairs to check on Penny. She's asleep. Sleeping like the dead, honestly. Good, she needs it. Coming off what sounds like decades of antipsychotic medication is going to be a bumpy ride, and a long-haul, at that.

I quietly close her curtains and close her door, standing in the hallway for a moment to try to make sense of everything that's happened in the last hour.

Dr. Ashford might die. He was stabbed repeatedly.

I remember the crimson ribbons in the sink a few nights ago and how, at first, I thought it had been blood.... And Dalton had been putting away a butcher knife at the exact moment I'd walked into the kitchen, too.

I swallow, finding it nearly impossible, and walk downstairs.

The house is quiet all around me when I walk back into the kitchen and chug my iced tea, which is now watered down and luke-warm. I pour myself another glass in hopes it'll wash the taste of bile from my mouth as I stand in front of the kitchen window.

There's a box in the yard that hadn't been there before. A black shoebox sitting right in the grass.

What the hell?

I look around for Curtis. He's nowhere to be seen. It's closing in on 5:00, so he wouldn't be here anyway. Maybe he forgot it, whatever it is?

I walk out on the back porch and look up at the sky and the fast moving dark clouds rolling in with the promise of more rain and more storms.

I glance back at the box, huffing out a breath.

I haven't been out here for a while, not since my ill-fated adventure through the swamp. I keep my eyes locked on the box and refuse to even look at the tree line as I make a beeline for it, the first droplets of rain from tonight's storm bouncing off the top of my head.

I pick it up, and it's light. Almost like it's totally empty, but a single shake tells me there's something small inside.

"Hmm..." I hum to myself as I examine the outside of the box before turning on my heel and carrying it back into the house. I set it on the kitchen table and back away, planting my hands on my hips.

I should be worried about whatever's in this random ass box. I have way too much to think about right now.

My fingertips prickle as I scan it, then I roll my eyes and stop forward, throwing the lid open.

I scream.

23

LAYLA

MY SCREAM PENETRATES the air as I stumble away from the table. I clasp my hands over my mouth, blood thrumming in my ears as my back hits the counter, and I can no longer retreat away from the box.

The smell of it... God, I can barely stand it. I gag, whirling to face the wall. Footsteps thunder in the hallway, and I turn to find Dalton skidding to a stop, his hands and shirt smeared with paint. "Layla?"

His eyes leave my face and snap to the box. He straightens, closing his eyes, and slowly nods to himself as he takes a deep breath and stalks toward the table.

"Stop!" I shout, but it's too late. He calmly closes the lid and tucks it under his arm before walking out the back door. "Dalton!"

"Stay inside, Layla!"

I reach the screen door and push it open just as he starts walking across the back yard toward the tree line. "Where are you.... What are you doing!?"

He whirls around with the box, his eyes narrowed on mine. "I said stay inside!"

I ignore his sharp tone and rush down the steps, chasing after him as he continues across the grass. "Dalton, stop! We have to call the police!"

"We're not calling the police. We're not doing shit, Layla. Go inside, right now." He growls the last two words, his tone pinched and deathly serious.

I shake my head, pointing to the box. "There's a fucking tongue in that box, Dalton!"

"I saw it," he says through gritted teeth.

"And a rose, and my–my name written in blood." I gag again. Normally, I have a stomach of steel thanks to my years of nursing, but this? "You haven't been leaving me roses, have you? It's not you. It wasn't you." I close my eyes and shake my head, my mind curling in on itself as I pull every memory of the last few weeks to the forefront. The roses, that creeping feeling of being watched, the man walking through the marsh the day I thought I was following Dalton…. "I'm being stalked, Dalton. I need to call the police!"

He reaches for me, but I flinch away. "Layla, look at me."

I turn to the house, but he grabs my arm. "Whose tongue is it?"

His eyes undergo a great change. He looks almost guilty, and then the pieces start falling into place.

"Oh, my God," I whisper, stepping out of his grasp. "Oh, my God, Dalton. You didn't!" I look at the box still propped under his arm and fight the urge to scream.

"Didn't what, Layla?"

"Whose tongue is that?" I ask again with more force.

"I don't know," he says sharply. "I'm going to get rid of it."

"The police–"

"Will not help you," he finishes for me, taking a single short step in my direction. "Don't bother."

"Why?"

"You know about the murders that took place here now. I heard you talking to Robert Wilson about it. But you don't know the half of it, Angel. This place is built from flesh and bones, from blood. The police won't touch this place. The police won't do anything about this; they won't help you. If anything, they'll turn this against you and have you locked up for insanity like every other woman who was unlucky enough to have ended up here!"

There's so much raw emotion in his voice. I stand completely still, shocked into silence. Dalton just stares at me, shaking his head.

"Do you realize how much danger you've been in since you came here?"

"What are you trying to say?"

He opens his mouth to reply but then shuts it again, his eyes leaving my face and narrowing on the back porch just as a car door slams. "It's-it's just Bailey-"

"Go back inside," he growls, "right now. Please, Layla, just listen to me for fucking once in your life!"

"Okay," I choke out just as Bailey's voice lifts through the air, calling out my name. I turn to the porch as she walks out, but then I turn back to Dalton.

He's gone, likely having disappeared into the tangled vine-coated tree line just a few steps away. I stare into the murky shadows of the swamp, wondering how the hell he moved so fast and out of sight, but then Bailey calls out my name again, asking, "What are you doing out here?"

"Getting some fresh air," I say, praying my words are calm and steady as I hug myself and turn toward her, walking briskly across the yard. I hope she didn't hear me scream earlier, but I think she just got back. "Did you find the doctor you were talking about?" I walk up the steps to meet her. She's holding a plastic bag of what smells like Chinese takeout in one hand and a casserole dish covered in tinfoil in the other.

"No, she wasn't home, but I called her practice in New Orleans, and they promised she'll come by tomorrow morning." She lifts the bag, tilting her head toward it. "I went out to get us some dinner."

"You don't have to stay with me tonight during my shift if you don't want to."

"I need to," she says with a soft smile. "Maybe it's just morbid curiosity, but Ms. Penny has never spoken to me like that, ever. I've heard her talking to herself over the monitor, but that's about it until now. Mom made us a casserole, but I'm not sure how good it is, so I stopped for Chinese as well.

"Thank you." I take the casserole dish from her and walk back into the house.

We sit down at the snug kitchen table to eat, periodically checking the cameras in Aunt Penny's room. "Did you find out anything about Dr. Ashford?"

Bailey nods grimly, grimacing down at her fried rice. "Yeah, I did. My mom's congregation is putting together a prayer circle for him today outside the hospital. He's brain-dead, Layla. He was stabbed in the throat, and it severed his spinal cord." She takes a breath. "Whoever did this to him was violent about it. His lungs collapsed and... they cut out his tongue.``

I nearly spit my mouthful of food on the table. "Wh-what?"

She nods, picking at her orange chicken with her fork. "He's going to die, that's clear. His wife is a mess. She won't see anyone. The police have his whole property taped off. I'm sure they'll catch whoever did it soon."

My stomach sinks as a sick, twisting feeling settles in my gut.

"I haven't done anything." Dalton's words flash through my mind from the night after the doctor assaulted me.

He'd been adamant I not call the police about the tongue in the box. Dr. Ashford's tongue.

I look past Bailey at the tree line, the whole backyard now cast in the soft glow of the beginning stages of the sunset. It's a clear, bright evening. Not a cloud in the sky. The soft rain shower from what feels like only moments ago moved off toward the coast in a matter of minutes.

Bailey sets her fork down and runs her hands over her face. "I'm going to run back into town for a few hours—go home and shower, and pack a bag for the night. I wanted to get back here as soon as I could with the food, so I didn't stop on my way back."

"I'll be fine," I assure her. "Take your time. If she wakes up, I'll just be careful around her if I still make her nervous."

"My guess," Bailey says as she stands, taking her plate with her, "is that she'll sleep all night, maybe into tomorrow. She has so much medication still running through her system. It might take several days for us to safely get her off all those strong medications."

Bailey and I clean up from dinner, and then she takes her leave. I watch her pull out of the driveway, the remaining shreds of golden sunset gleaming on the roof of her car as it bumps down the driveway.

I turn to the stairs, suddenly exhausted, and begin to climb, my mind reeling over every possibility. Did Dalton do this? If so, why would he leave the tongue for me to find with other grisly little gifts and then act so strange about me finding it?

Nothing makes sense.

I push open the door to my room and step inside with every intention of falling face first onto the mattress when I find Dalton sitting on the edge of my bed, his head turned to the window. Golden light plays over the sharp lines of his cheeks and jaw as he slowly turns his gaze to meet mine.

I close the door behind me and lock it. The digital clock on my bedside table says 8:30 P.M. I'm not sure when Bailey will be back, but Dalton and I need to talk.

Now.

"Did you break into Dr. Ashford's house and try to kill him?"

"No."

I press my back to the door. I'm not letting him leave without answers. He stands, tucking his hands in his pockets and turns to face me fully.

"Did you put that tongue in the box and leave it for me to find?"

"No, I did not."

"But you–"

"If I had wanted to kill Dr. Ashford for what he did to you," he says, his tone low and dangerous, "and trust me, Layla, I wanted to, I wouldn't have stabbed him. I wouldn't have cut out his tongue." He edges closer to me, his proximity making the fine, downy hairs on the back of my neck rise to attention. "I wouldn't have done it that way. It was sloppy, in my opinion. He deserved a lot more than he got."

"How would you have done it?" I can't believe the words that fall from my lips. I also can't believe I'm wet right now, but Dalton's predatory gaze rakes over me, fixing on my neck, and my rising pulse.

His mouth ticks into a sly smile. "Do you really want to know?"

He cages me in against the door, his forearm resting above my head while his other hand travels up my waist. "Yes," I whisper, closing my eyes as his touch sends sparks of desire over my skin.

"I would have brought him here, Angel, and taken him apart piece by piece. I would have flayed his skin from his body while he still breathed. And then…." He brushes the words over the rim of my ear. "Then, I would have given you the knife, and let you be the one to cut out his tongue." Dalton's tongue darts out, sliding down my neck. "Then, I would have strung up whatever was left of him in the middle of downtown where everyone would have to bear witness to him and they would know what that son of a bitch did to my girl."

My legs tremble, but his hand on my waist keeps me steady as he sucks on the delicate skin between my neck and shoulder, drawing a moan from my lips.

I'm finding it hard to focus, especially when his hand slides from my waist to the juncture of my thighs. "Dalton–"

"Shh…" he whispers, applying delicious pressure between my legs.

"If it wasn't you, then who was it?"

"Someone that wants what they can never have. You're mine, Layla."

He presses me hard against the door, his body flush with mine.

"I think I need to remind you who you belong to."

24

LAYLA

DALTON'S HAND slides up my side under my shirt, his rough, calloused hand smoothing over my skin. I shiver against his touch, my eyes fluttering closed.

"Come with me," he whispers against my neck, sucking the delicate skin hard enough to leave a bruise.

I'll follow him anywhere. That's how I know I'm in deep, drowning in him, actually. I'll follow him to hell if he asks.

Maybe I'm already there.

A gentle scratching noise sounds overhead as he guides me into the bathroom, his eyes locked on mine, dark and full of primal heat. Desire. Excitement.

I look up at the ceiling as the scratching sound gets louder, like something is scurrying back and forth right above us.

"Eyes on me," he whispers, and I look back at him, nodding as if in a trace.

He shuts the bathroom door behind us, his fingers still intertwined with mine. "Dalton?"

"Shh…." He turns to me, caging me in against the counter. "Don't say anything, Angel. Just let me take your mind off everything."

That sounds perfect. I'm already under his spell when he lets go of my hand and turns to the shower. In a matter of seconds, steam feels the snug room, the hot water thrumming against the tiles.

He turns back to me slowly. My heart bears erratically as his gaze rakes over my body. "Take off your clothes," he commands, his voice low and rasping.

I slowly pull my shirt over my head, tossing it to the ground. He inhales sharply, his eyes traveling down from my face to my neck, then my lacy blue bra. I keep my eyes on his face as I hook my thumbs in my shorts and shimmy out of them, standing in nothing but my bra and a matching thong.

"Everything, Angel," he says. He watches my hands as I pull down my thong, then I reach behind my back to unclasp my bra.

Steam swirls around my skin while I stand in front of him, bared to him, my blood roaring through my ears. I step toward him and guide his shirt over his head, then reach for his belt.

His knuckles graze over my upper breasts as I undo his jeans and shove them down over his muscular thighs. He seems to be in just as much of a trance as I am when I kneel, pulling his boxers down.

He told me I belong to him. I want him to treat me like it.

Kneeling, I rest my hands on his thighs, looking up at him. I open my mouth and stick out my tongue.

A cocky smirk plays over his lips. He chuckles darkly down at me while running his fingers through my hair to cup the back of my head. His cock is rigid as I slide my hands up his thighs. Slowly, he drags the head over my tongue, exhaling deeply.

I wait for his praise; I'm desperate for it.

I open my mouth wider in invitation for him to fuck my mouth. A faint mewling whimper escapes my throat as he teases his cock against my tongue, giving me only a taste of him. Salty, sweet, every-thing I've been craving.

"You," he rasps, gripping the back of my head with more force, "are a very good girl, Angel."

I close my eyes and moan as he thrusts his dick into my mouth, hitting the back of my throat. I suck him down, grazing my teeth down his shaft.

Looking up at him, I notice he's closed his eyes, his lips slightly parted as he pumps into my mouth and drags his cock out slowly, relishing the way my tongue swirls over the head.

"Layla." He whispers my name like a prayer. It sends shivers of pleasure licking down my spine and settling between my thighs.

I suck him down again, further than ever before, my vision going blurry at the edges as that fight or flight response kicks in. I can't breathe around his girth. His length glides down my throat, and I fight against my gag reflex, willing myself to relax.

I am his. I belong to him—and only him.

And right now, I want him to know that he is mine.

He pulls out all the way, looking down at me with a sleepy, heated expression. It's a soft look, something I realize he doesn't show often.

I don't know this man. I don't know anything about his childhood, his family, or his life beyond this house. But I know that there's something different about this... the feelings between us. His body feels like it was made for mine, and his touch is the one thing that's ever been able to set my soul aflame.

He taps the head of his cock on my outstretched tongue. "You're so beautiful with my dick in your mouth."

I'm so wet that I'm dripping down my thighs.

He takes me by the wrists and pulls me upright, roughly pressing me against the counter. The shower stills runs in the background as he spins me around so I'm facing the mirror. His paint smeared hands wipe away the mist clinging to the glass, and then I'm staring at my reflection while he stands behind me, his hands coming up around my belly to cup my breasts, which are full and aching to be touched.

I close my eyes and moan, pressing my ass on his thighs. "I need you."

"Open your eyes, Angel. I want you to watch while I fuck you."

One of his hands grazes up to my neck, squeezing lightly. I open my eyes just as he presses his dick against my entrance, sliding it through the wet heat gathered there. I gasp at the fullness as his head penetrates my pussy.

"Are you sore, Angel?" he whispers, against my hair. I watch through the reflection in the mirror as he nudges my head to the side, giving him access to my neck.

He groans in my ear as he thrusts into my pussy, my belly pressed against the counter. He fills me up completely and hisses through his teeth at the way my pussy tightens around his cock. I lift up on my toes so I can take him deeper.

This isn't like the times before. There is something far more intimate about the way he's touching me now. Even while he's fucking me from behind, his hands leaves my neck. One cups my breast, the other one resting on my hip as he closes his eyes and presses his forehead to the top of my head. He grits his teeth like he's holding back.

"Open your eyes," I tell him, unable to recognize my own voice. It's low and sultry, exuding a kind of confidence I hadn't realized I possessed.

He slowly raises his head, his eyes washed in ecstasy, and meets my eyes in the mirror.

My lips part in a moan as I keep my eyes on his, my climax beginning to curl through my lower belly and into my thighs. The tension builds, getting sharper and deeper with each thrust.

I want Dalton unleashed. I want him to scream my name. I want him whispering his praise in my ear while I come undone with his cock buried in my pussy.

His eyes darken as he nips the rim of my ear, his eyes still locked on mine. "Your pussy is fucking paradise, Angel. The way you grip me…." He growls low in his throat, his lips dipping from my ear to my neck, his teeth grazing over my pulse. "Do you like watching yourself get fucked?"

"Only by you." My eyes nearly roll back in my head when he hits that spot deep inside of me that sends my heart rate skyrocketing.

He chuckles low in his throat, raking his teeth over my shoulder. His hand leaves my breast and travels over my belly, then to where we're joined. I whimper when his fingers brush over my clit in rough circles, the feeling ripples through me and causes me to clamp down around his cock.

"Oh, that's it," he moans, biting down on my shoulder. His teasing touch is light, soft, less than what I need to come, and he knows it.

I arch my hips, taking him deeper, my mouth parting in another whimper as my legs start to shake.

He pumps into me hard, the sound of our bodies joining echoing through the room.

"Dalton–" I choke out. I'm close. So, so close. I just need a little more. I want more.

"Beg," he says in my ear, and I practically scream his name as he pulls out all the way and slams into me again.

"Please!" I cry out. His thrusts become violent, damning; the counter bites into my stomach as he pounds home, filling me wholly and completely. He slaps my clit, causing me to scream his name again, and again, his cock dragging in and out of my sore and swollen pussy.

He hooks an arm around me, clutching my back to his chest, and presses a rough kiss to my neck.

Then I'm coming undone, falling to pieces in his arms. My legs shake violently as the strongest orgasm I've ever felt in my entire life rips through my body. Stars fill my vision, and I gasp for breath. My pussy spasms around his dick, but he's not done. He pulls out, whirling me around so we're chest to chest, and then lifts me up onto the counter and spreads my legs wide.

He thrusts into me again, his mouth crushed to mine. I wrap my arms around his neck and hold on for dear life.

"Dalton," I whisper against his lips.

"Angel," he replies, breathless.

"You're mine."

He looks into my eyes as he comes, buried deep inside of me.

His tongue sweeps over my lower lip, then his mouth is on mine again in a kiss so passionate, it takes my breath away.

I expect him to leave, for whatever reason. I expect to spend the rest of the evening alone, like usual. But gently, he helps me off the counter and guides me into the shower, where his hands travel over every inch of my body, and his mouth finds mine again and again.

It's only a matter of minutes before he's hard once more, and his touch becomes more frenzied. Before I know it, my back is pressed against the wall, and he's holding me up, my legs locked around his waist, while he fucks me dizzy.

The entire time, his lips are on mine, soft and passionate, the kisses full of something other than possession. Feeling, I believe. Connection. An emotion maybe neither of us are ready to put into words.

Because... well, what happens after this? Do we have a future together outside of this creepy house and fucked up situation?

Do we have an out, somehow?

Or is what I feel for him only the need for comfort and distraction?

Either way, an hour later, I'm getting dressed, and Dalton is walking out my bedroom door. He looks at me over his shoulder, that cocky smile that I love playing over his lips before he says, "I'll find you later."

"You're absolutely insatiable," I remark.

He winks at me, which he's never done before, and it sets a spark of hope flaming to life in my heart.

"Only for you."

The door closes with a soft click, and I'm alone. Beyond the windows, night has fallen. I dress in my usual scrubs, ready for whatever the night will bring with Aunt Penny, and wait for Bailey to come back.

My head is clear, and I'm ready for whatever happens next.

But then a long, jagged scraping sound echoes above my head, muffled by the ceiling and floorboards above me. I look up, wondering if the calm, starry weather outside is enough of a shelter from the storm brewing inside of the house tonight with each passing second.

25

LAYLA

BAILEY'S EYES are growing heavy despite the third cup of coffee she's consumed in the last two hours. We're in the supply room, years and years of notes taken by a variety of nurses spread out on the plastic table between us. She brings the coffee to her lips, shaking her head. "What are we going to do?"

"Nothing until your doctor friend gets here tomorrow," I tell her, swiveling from side to side in the computer chair while the printer beside me works in overdrive. We've been going through the computer system, printing out everything and anything pertaining to Aunt Penny's care. The notes only go back ten years or so, but that should be enough to give this new doctor a clear idea of what's been done to her.

"What about Vera?" Bailey asks, her eyes rimmed red with fatigue.

"I'll handle Vera this weekend. I'm going to call the lawyer after we talk to this new doctor and fill him in on everything, then I'll have Curtis come over and change the locks." In my opinion, Vera has no right to ever step foot in this house again, especially if she conspired with Dr. Ashford to keep Aunt Penny in a state of full mental sedation for what sounds like decades.

But, I do want to know why she did it.

I cross my arms and lean back, watching Bailey peer over the notes. "Bailey, just go to bed. Aunt Penny isn't going to wake up tonight; we both know it. My bed is made up. Go sleep there." She's not used to working nights, and it shows.

"All right." She sighs, giving me a soft smile. "But wake me up if anything happens."

"I will, don't worry."

She stands with a groan and pads away, disappearing into the shadowy stairwell. I swivel back to the computer and print out a few more notes then spend the next half hour organizing everything in neat piles on the table. The tablet with a video feed of Aunt Penny's room is silent, and she's asleep.

In fact, it's surprisingly quiet in the house tonight. The open windows let in a soft, cool breeze, and the air is full of the songs of cicadas and frogs.

For once, the house doesn't feel full of ghosts. And for once, I feel calm and secure within its walls and not exceedingly on edge.

Also, my body is still thrumming with bliss from my encounter with Dalton earlier this evening.

I smile to myself as I walk into the kitchen for a snack and another cup of coffee. I wonder where he is right now. He's likely painting or sleeping. I realize I've never really ever sought him out. He always seems to just appear out of nowhere.

For a moment, all I want to do is go find him, maybe sit in his studio for a minute and watch him work, but... this thing between us is just physical, right?

I have to be okay with it if it is just physical between us. I can't catch feelings for him, even though it feels impossible not to. We haven't ever talked about what this is between us. We don't talk about much at all, actually.

Maybe it's better this way–just a bit of summer fun.

A soft scratching sound catches my attention while I rinse my mug out in the kitchen sink. The scratching is similar to what I've heard in the house many times before but have always done my best to ignore. This time, it's a distant sound, like it's coming from outside. I stare out the window, narrowing my eyes on the shadows along the tree line. Did I see something move, or is it just another trick of my mind?

The scratching sound grows sharper, echoing across the yard as I step out on the back porch.

It's probably just raccoons, like Curtis said. There's several outbuildings scattered around the more developed parts of the property, many of which are run-down and unused as far as I know.

Something heavy falls somewhere past the trees to my left where several sheds fan out in the overgrowth.

Huffing out a breath, I turn back to the house and grab a flashlight and a knife from the kitchen before stalking out. My sandals crunch through the grass, then hit the back driveway, and I stop, waiting for the sound to come again.

A scurrying, scraping sound comes from one of the sheds near a cluster of trees.

I walk around the back of the detached garage and fan my flashlight through the trees. One of the sheds is open, and as I point my flashlight through the door, I find nothing but gardening supplies stacked neatly on old wooden shelves.

The scratching sound comes again–like nails on a chalkboard. "Where the hell is that coming from?"

I whirl toward the trees. A crumbling structure withers into the brush only a few yards past the tree line, obscured by shadows. The scratching sound is coming from within it.

I immediately bristle with fear. First of all, why am I out here, anyway? I look down at the knife in my hand. What the hell was I thinking?

But curiosity gets the better of me as I creep toward the building, my flashlight lighting the way forward as I step between the trees and shove my way through the brush.

I push open the door, which creaks so loudly it sends an echo through the yard and over the standing water where the marsh begins.

It's pitch black inside, empty, and cold. I step over the threshold and peer around, the light from my flashlight dusting over cobweb covered crates and old shelving.

There's a wall made of brick–sloppily constructed–toward the back of the room. It looks odd against the rotting wood sides of the outbuilding. A few of the bricks have come loose, some of them lying on the ground in front of the wall.

I wait in silence, my heart in my throat, for anything to happen. A sound, a shadow....

A sharp scratch echoes through the space. I whirl toward the brick wall and flash my light against it. There's something behind it. My light catches a gleam of an object, white and smooth.

My senses take over as I grip the knife and walk forward. The scratching sound suddenly intensifies, as does a creeping, desperate sensation now crippling my mind. Frantically, I begin to stab my knife between the bricks, loosening some of them, then drop the knife to start pulling the bricks out of the wall with one hand as I hold the flashlight with the other.

My breath comes in quick gasps as my nails scrape over the bricks, pulling them free, letting them hit the ground at my feet.

The scratching sound is louder than ever, so loud my ears pop and ring. I pull another brick free and half the wall comes down. I step back just in time, sucking in a breath full of dust and... decay.

A half rotted body slumps forward, one hand outstretched like it's reaching for me, it's fingers worn down to the bone.

The bricks at my feet are covered in scratch marks like...like whoever this is had been trying to scratch their way out–

I rest my hands on my knees as the smell hits me–rancid and overwhelming. Bile rises in my throat as I squeeze my eyes shut.

"Layla?"

My name brushes over my cheek and causes my skin to prickle with terror. I open my eyes, and the dead man is directly beneath me, his eyes milky and wide open as his half decayed mouth parts. "Layla!"

My scream rips through the air as I stagger backward, groping in the dark for anything to break my fall. My flashlight clatters to the ground and flickers out, casting me in darkness.

I fall backward over the threshold of the building into the woods, landing hard on my ass just as a shadow roams over me. Another scream tears from my throat before a hand claps over my mouth.

"It's just me."

"Dalton!" I choke against the palm of his hand. He pulls me upright, checking me for any injuries. "Dalton!"

"Why are you out here? Have you not listened to anything I've said–"

"There's a body," I sob, my voice cracking over the words. "Daltons, there's a dead person in there!"

He takes my face between his hands, looking hard into my eyes. "Eyes on me, Angel."

I whimper, choking down a sob. "I'm dreaming–I'm dreaming again, aren't I?"

He says nothing, but the look in his eyes is absolutely heartbreaking as he shakes his head. "Come on," he whispers, wrapping an arm around my shoulder. "I'm putting you to bed."

"But the body–"

My knees give out, but he catches me, scooping me up into his arms and cradling me to his chest like I'm a small child. "Don't worry about it now."

"Did you know?"

"No," he grinds out. "I didn't."

"Who is it?"

He shushes me with a gentleness I hadn't expected from him. He carries me across the yard and into the house just as clouds begin to flood the sky, covering the stars. "The knife–I left a knife in there."

"I'm going to take care of it," Dalton whispers as he carries me through the kitchen.

He walks upstairs but passes my door where Bailey is sleeping. Instead, he climbs another flight of stairs and edges toward the door to his room, still carrying me in his arms.

He must know Bailey is asleep in my bed. Or, he wants me here, close by.

He sets me on the edge of the bed and pulls my shirt over my head.

"Your pants, too."

"Why?"

"Because you're filthy," he growls, making a little clicking sound with his tongue. He leaves me to undress and disappears into his bathroom, and within seconds, I hear a shower running and cabinets opening and closing. "Take a shower and then go to bed. Do not leave this room."

For once, I obey and let the hot shower scald me while I rub my skin raw.

Dalton isn't in the room when I leave the bathroom wrapped in a towel. His door is firmly closed, locked, in fact, from the outside.

I wiggle the knob, my heart rate spiking.

That bastard locked me in here.

Exhaustion and shock keep my senses blurred as I move to the window on the far side of the room. My view of the backyard is blocked by the garage, and the shed is just out of sight. Where did he go? What does he mean to do with the body I found?

He won't call the police, I'm sure.

I slide into his bed wondering if I can trust him. I want to. I feel like, in a way, I need to trust this man.

If he were going to hurt me, he would have done so already.

I slip into sleep so quickly I'm unaware it's happening. Darkness clouds my mind–the inky, black kind that promises a long, dreamless rest.

What feels like hours later, I wake slowly, sleepily, to the feeling of someone pressed against me. A familiar scent hits me, and I think it has to be Dalton. Naked beneath the sheets, I press my body to his, my eyes still closed, my breath coming in a soft rasp. He slides his arm under my neck, his other arm resting under my breasts. He nuzzles my neck, then my ear, his teeth lighting grazing the rim.

It feels wicked and loving at the same time.

26

DALTON

AFTER I PUT Layla to bed, I return immediately to the shed. I look down at the dead man with a mix of pity and rage. He's not much older than me. He was handsome, with blond hair and eyes that used to be blue. But now, they've started to decay into his skull. The skin is flayed from his fingers, revealing bone, but the rest of him is in surprisingly good shape considering how long he's been here.

I remember him. Henry, that was his name. Henry Swanson, from Mississippi, an architect apprentice who never made it back after traveling here to visit his girlfriend.

The last night nurse.

I wrap a bandana around my nose and mouth and crouch, picking up the knife Layla discarded upon discovering the poor bastard.

That's what he is, too. Discarded. This wasn't his fault.

I wonder what was going through that young nurse's head as she put each brick in place. A glance at his torso tells me she stabbed him at least once, somewhere that caused him a great deal of blood loss, enough to effectively knock him out long enough for her to cage him into this tomb.

But he hadn't stayed like that.

I wrap the putrid body in a tarp, trying not to breathe. His hand slips out, his bones gleaming in the light of the lantern I brought with me. The missing skin from his fingers exposes the bone. I imagine he did that to himself as he'd been trying to claw his way out.

I drag the body out to the marsh, trudging through still water. Rain peppers the top of my head as I walk forever until I reach the edge of the woods and reach the expansive wetlands that choke the Gregory property.

Something out here will eat what's left of this body, regardless of its level of decay. I unroll the tarp and let the body splash into the water. Airless, it slips away into the murky depths, never to be seen again.

Sitting on a ledge that overlooks the water, sheltered from the rain with my back resting against a tree, I watch the rain dust over the wetlands as I draw a cigarette from my pocket and light it, dragging the smoke down my throat before letting it out slowly.

The poor woman who did this likely didn't realize what she'd done until it was too late. She killed this man out of fear, but it wasn't his fault. It was never any of their faults.

"Was it fun?" I ask the endless marsh around me. "Did you enjoy tormenting her until she snapped?"

I'm answered by silence. Amos has been quiet since Ms. Penny woke up from her stupor. He's leery of her, of course. She is the last of the Gregorys who were able to keep this beast contained, and without her in the picture, he was allowed decades of torture, almost always ending in murder.

The previous night nurse had no idea Amos was whispering in her head. She had no idea until she killed the man she loved and ran desperate into the woods to get away from the real threat in that house.

When I came to this place, I had no idea what would be waiting for me. But, unlike the rest of the men and women who've had the displeasure of walking those shadowed halls, I've lived in houses before that were inhabited by otherworldly beings.

Amos can't tempt me. He can't pierce my mind and make me act out, doing his bidding. He can't force me to rape and torture like he'd forced these other men to do.

But he's in Layla's head. I know it. And if he's not, he's getting close. His only desire is to make her fearful of me, to make me out to be the bad guy, to make her believe I'd hurt her so she'll hurt me in return.

I can do all of that by myself. I don't need his help. Which is why he hasn't driven her to madness yet.

I take another drag from my cigarette and toss it into the marsh. Curious fish inspect it but dart away, disappearing back into the gloom.

By the time I make it back to the house, it's pouring down rain. Thunder booms in the distance, echoing through the house as I slowly make my way upstairs. I'm soaking wet and tired and completely forgot I'd put Layla to bed in my room a few hours ago. I pause in the doorway, then shut the door, walking back to the second floor.

I check on Ms. Penny first. She's asleep, her room cast in silver shadows as the storm starts to move closer to the house.

Next, I check on the other nurse. Bailey is curled in a little ball in Layla's bed. I stand in the doorway for several long seconds watching her sleep. She shouldn't have stayed the night here.

Slowly, I close the door and return to my own room to shower.

Lightning illuminates the sky when I finally slide into bed beside Layla, her body warm, supple, and bare in my hands as I pull her to my chest.

I have the unmistakable urge to claim her as I lower my face to her shoulder, inhaling her soft scent now tinged with my citrus shampoo.

If I'd been a weaker man, Amos would have both of us in his clutches. We wouldn't have lasted this long, either. But maybe that's a bad thing. This push and pull with him the last several weeks since Layla's arrival has only made him more desperate to consume her, to take over her mind, to try to force her to take care of his biggest problems.

Being trapped in this house—and me.

I push my knee between her thighs and clutch her to my chest, my arm snaking under her neck while my free hand clutches her breasts, gently kneading while my mind spins over every possibility of escape that we have.

I can't think of any.

She lets out her breath in a soft moan, her nipples hardening under my touch. Her heat slides over my thigh as she grinds her pussy into my leg. She's barely awake, but it's not the first time I've taken her while she slept.

"Is this what you want?" I whisper, my lips brushing her ear as I gently nudge her legs apart and fist my cock, teasing her entrance. I roll her from her side to her belly, and her ass beckons to me–round and soft and perfect. She's an excellent distraction. Maybe that's what Amos wants her to be for me–something to keep my attention diverted. It works. My mind is completely consumed by Layla to the point I can barely think straight, let alone paint. Every time I close my eyes, I see her. Her safety and wellbeing has completely consumed me.

But I made Amos a deal several years ago, a deal he continues to hold over my head. The only request I've ever made of him is to give me Layla. Yet, he keeps fucking with her.

"Layla," I whisper, kissing the back of her neck as I press my cock inside of her. Her pussy clutches my dick in a way that makes my head spin. Every inch of her is perfect.

Her answering moan has me pumping into her with fervor, loving the way she clamps and spasms as she comes in pounding waves.

It doesn't take long. Layla's body reacts to mine in a way I've never experienced with anyone else. She is made for me.

And I'll die before I let anyone, or anything, else have her.

27

LAYLA

I WAKE up in Dalton's bed around 5:00 in the morning, and he is no longer there, of course. I have no idea where his studio is located in the tangle of hallways on the third floor. It's the only place I assume he'd be right now.

The house is quiet as I pad downstairs after checking on my aunt and Bailey, both of which are still asleep. I go through my normal morning routine. I'm wearing nothing but a pair of boy shorts and one of Dalton's shirts. I smell like him, which makes me think of him, and thinking of him makes me wonder if I'm falling in too deep with a man I barely know.

I make a pot of coffee and pour myself a mug before stepping out onto the back porch to watch the sky turn from a dark gray to a pale silver, but as the morning shadows stretch across the grass, memories of last night come flooding back to the forefront of my mind.

I clutch my mug so tight my knuckles turn white as I slowly turn my gaze toward the outbuildings where the early morning light casts heavy shadows in the trees.

I can't stop myself from walking out into the grass and across the yard, the rain-wet ground cool against my bare feet. My mind goes numb, some deep, morbidly curious part of me controlling my actions as I walk to the dilapidated building where I found a body the night before.

I stand at the threshold and look into the shadows, the morning light illuminating the scattered bricks now lying on the dust covered ground.

The body is gone.

Which means Dalton did something with it.

I'm not sure what to think about that.

I walk back to the house with every intention of finding him and asking what he did with the body when I hear a soft alarm beeping somewhere in the house.

I check the video feed on the tablet in the supply room. Aunt Penny's awake, sitting up in bed, her eyes taking in her surroundings.

"Oh, no," I grumble, turning for the stairs.

I should wake up Bailey. I shouldn't even be considering going into Penny's room on my own, not after what happened, but…

"Good morning," I say kindly, my smile warm and inviting as I slowly edge into the room. I shut the door behind me before walking further inside.

Penny watches each step I take, her deep blue eyes clear, cold, and locked on my face. She's lost the weak, frail look about her. Now, with less and less sedatives coursing through her system, she's sharp and stern, her face a mask of ice.

"I'm Layla Bryant. I'm your night nurse." I walk to the side of her bed to check the ECG machine. Everything looks fine. "How're you feeling this morning? Can I get you anything?"

I look down at her, trying not to flinch under her steely gaze. She asks, "Who are you?"

"Layla–"

"No, not your name."

I realize what she's asking. She looks me up and down, frowning at my outfit and bare feet.

"We're related, actually. My mom's name is Trudy Bryant... Trudy Gregory."

Her coldly appraising gaze locks on my face again. "You shouldn't be here."

"Can you–can you tell me why?"

To my surprise, and horror, if I'm being honest, her thin mouth ticks into a haunting smile. I expect her to say something about how the house is haunted, and the murders, and the sordid history of this place that drove my line of the family to keep its distance. "Where's the other nurse?"

"Bailey is still asleep. Her shift doesn't normally start until nine–"

"No. Vera." Her voice is cold as she sits up a little straighter, her finely boned fingers smoothing the sheets over her lap.

"She only works on the weekends."

"She's not allowed on this property any longer. Am I understood?" Her eyes, so much like my own, meet mine.

I nod, resisting the urge to sink into a seated position on the edge of her bed and ask her if she knows she's been kept sedated for what sounds like many years, if not decades. "How do I prevent that from happening?"

"Who hired you, girl?"

"Mr. Hart. Your lawyer."

"I don't know a Mr. Hart," she says harshly. "Where is Mr. Mason?"

"I don't know who that is."

"Then call this Mr. Hart and tell him I'm awake and that I need to speak to him. Look at this place." She sweeps a trembling hand around the finely dressed room as if it's falling to decay all around us.

"Uhm, Ms. Penny?"

"What?"

I lick my lips, heaving a sigh as I edge closer to the bed. "We have a new doctor coming to assess you today. Is that all right?"

She rolls her eyes to the ceiling. "Does it look like I have much of a choice, girl? I've been bedridden against my will for years. It's not like I can get up and walk away."

"Ms. Penny… Aunt Penny, yesterday you saw me…" I trail off, unsure of how to phrase what I need to say. "You told me I needed to get out before it's too late. What did you mean?"

"If you didn't know what I'm talking about, you have no reason to worry."

I furrow my brows at her. "But–"

She suddenly breaks her gaze from the ceiling and slowly looks back into my eyes, the sharpness giving way to milky confusion. I back away a step, loosening my shoulders as her face screws up in a confused expression. "Who are you? Where is Vera?"

I nod, giving her a soft smile. *Dementia*, I remind myself. *She has Dementia.* These moments of lucidity are going to be fleeting, even without all the sedatives pumping through her system.

"I'll go get her," I lie, knowing it's all I can say. Penny lies back down against the cushions, her eyes on the ceiling as she takes a ragged breath.

"Amos," she breathes, and a chill snakes up my spine.

I've heard her say it before, but for whatever reason, this time the name sounds like a warning.

I try not to think about it as I leave the room, shutting the door firmly behind me. I find Bailey exiting my bedroom dressed in a pair of fresh scrubs.

"How did she do last night?"

"Fine," I tell her, swallowing past the lump in my throat. "She, uh, well, I was just talking to her, actually. She had a few very brief moments of lucidity just now, but I think she wore herself out." I tell her how Penny lost track of the conversation and asked me who I was then asked for Vera.

"The new doctor should be here in an hour, tops. She just texted me and asked if it would be all right to come over this morning before she has to head to the hospital in New Orleans."

"I think that's perfect. Then we can get in touch with Mr. Hart about everything else that's been going on."

Bailey nods her agreement, but her usually sunny expression cracks a bit as she runs a hand over her face.

"Are you all right?" I ask, stepping closer to her.

"I didn't sleep well," she says with a little laugh. "I had some weird…weird dreams last night."

My blood runs cold. "What kind of dreams?"

She blushes deeply, shaking her head. "Uh, it's nothing. I just–I had a weird feeling I wasn't alone. I guess I'm just not used to sleeping here, that's all."

"Sure," I say, trying not to reach out and throttle more information out of her. That's how all of this started, isn't it? Weird dreams. Lewd dreams that made me feel slightly violated yet desperate for more.

"I'm going to go get a cup of coffee. You should get some rest. I'll let you know what the doctor says."

"Okay," I say, fighting for a smile as she turns for the stairs.

In two steps, I'm back in my room. I close the door behind me and lean against it, my heart fluttering erratically.

Why do I suddenly feel like Bailey's in danger?

~

"I'M NOT sure what you're implying, Miss Bryant," Mr. Hart, the lawyer for the Gregory estate, drawls. Bailey is upstairs tending to Penny while I swivel back and forth in the computer chair, my arms crossed under my breasts as I look down at my phone, which is on speaker.

"Dr. Ashford overprescribed several heavy duty sedatives without reason which caused a prolonged state of psychosis in an elderly patient with dementia." I've spent the last twenty minutes explaining what the new doctor told us, and it was damning.

The medications likely did irreversible damage to Penny's already fragile psyche. She's frail, sickly, and bedridden. Her medications weren't necessary in the slightest. It did much more harm than good.

"And you're saying she didn't need it?"

"Yes," I practically growl. "And we believe Vera was in on it for whatever reason."

"What reason would either of them have to keep her in a state of near full sedation without medical cause?"

"That's why I'm calling you," I reply, rolling my eyes to the ceiling. "Is Vera in her will?"

"I... no, I don't believe so. Her will hasn't been updated since the nineties. Are you wondering if you're to inherit–"

"That's not what I'm getting at."

"Good because the house will go to the historical society upon Ms. Penny's passing, of that I'm certain. So how can I help you today, Miss Bryant?"

"She doesn't want Vera here anymore. She told me so herself."

"But she has dementia and clearly isn't in the right state of mind to make those kinds of decisions."

"She was very clear," I reiterate coldly, holding my ground. "Bailey and I aren't comfortable with it either."

"Fine, that's fine. Especially since she needs to find a new doctor anyway."

"She has a new doctor. In fact, Bailey is taking her to New Orleans in a few days for a full physical and to discuss options related to continued care. Penny needs to be in an assisted living home, Mr. Hart. It would be the best thing for her."

"I'd have to discuss that with the executor of her estate."

"So that's not you?" I'm confused again.

"I am her lawyer, and I was assigned to her when the last lawyer overseeing the estate and its financial holdings retired. The executor is court appointed, a professional. I'll handle it, but I'll need to speak to this new doctor before anything can be set in motion regarding moving her."

I turn to the left and see a shadow crossing the foyer. For a moment, I think it's Dalton, but there's no sound save for Mr. Hart's voice filling the space. My skin prickles with unease as I look around. It's late afternoon. Bailey is almost finished with her shift and planning on going home tonight. Helen Wilson recently dropped off the prescriptions the new doctor prescribed, all of which are only to help Penny sleep as she withdraws from her heavy sedatives.

"Miss Bryant?"

"Yes, sorry?"

"I said, is there anything else I can do for you today?"

"Oh," I say, my eyes still locked on the foyer. "Yeah, actually." I think about how he'd mentioned that the house will go to the historical society when Aunt Penny dies. What will happen to Dalton? "How long has Penny been allowing boarders at her property?"

"I'm sorry?"

"Boarders, like the artist who lives here. Dalton–"

"No one lives at the house besides Ms. Gregory. We've never allowed rooms to be rented, if that's what you're asking. Why? Who is Dalton–"

My heart sinks into my stomach. "Oh, never mind. I have–I have to go. Thank you for your time." I hang up before he can say another word.

Dalton isn't supposed to be here.

My mind drifts over the memories of Bailey and Vera not knowing who I was talking about when I mentioned him, and how Dalton refused to call the police when he found the tongue, and how he never called the police when we found the body...

I rise from the chair and rush toward the stairs.

<h1 align="center">28</h1>

———

LAYLA

"LAYLA!"

I skid to a stop in the hallway between my bedroom and Aunt Penny's room. Bailey shuts Aunt Penny's door with a soft click and beams at me. I force a smile to my lips, but it wobbles as she looks me up and down.

"I'm headed out. She's asleep. She'll probably sleep all night, I'm guessing. I'm going to take off, but I'll see you in the morning. Did you talk to the lawyer?"

"Yeah," I manage to choke out, but my mind is reeling, and my throat tightens as I continue. "He's going to talk to the estate executor about the assisted living home the doctor mentioned."

"Oh, that's good news," Bailey says with a sigh of relief. "She'd do so much better there. Anyway, I'm glad I caught you before you left because I just got a call from my mom."

"Oh, yeah?"

Bailey's sunny expression shifts to one of muted shock as she blows out her breath. "Dr. Ashford died."

"Oh, damn," I mumble, swallowing hard. "That's–that's a shame."

"They arrested the person who did it a few hours ago. It hasn't gone public yet…"

My heart nearly stops. Oh, God. When was the last time I saw Dalton? Last night, when he woke me up in the middle of the night to have sex? I'm barely keeping a handle on my nerves as I try to focus on what Bailey's saying, but the blood is hammering so loudly in my ears that all I can see is her mouth moving, her voice drowned out by the fear and confusion gripping my senses.

"Wh-what?" I stammer.

"His wife," Bailey says, her eyes going wide. "His wife did it! She killed him. She said he attacked her, and it was in self-defense. She's lost her mind entirely, according to my mom. She was transferred to an institution in New Orleans for now. I guess she had a psychotic break during the interview with the police and tried to stab herself in the neck with a ballpoint pen."

"Oh my God," I whisper, and that's all I can think to say.

"Anyway, I'll see you tomorrow!"

"B-Bye," I murmur, my heart threatening to leap out of my chest. I feel like I'm losing my goddamn mind as I rush up the steps to the third floor. I'm not sure my heart keeps beating as I skip every other step all the way to the top.

Dalton's bedroom door is locked. I bang on it, my chest squeezing tight with each rushed breath I take. I listen for footsteps, but I'm met by silence.

"Dalton?" I force out his name in a soft whisper like I'm afraid to say it any louder.

I turn to look down the darkened hallway and grip the banister to help guide my way through the dark. The hallway splits into a T. Light pours from a closed door down a hallway to the left. I suck in a breath, fighting to get my nerves in order before storming down the hall and throwing open the door with so much force it bounces off the wall.

Dalton's studio fans out in front of me. The air is stolen from my lungs as I step inside and look around, taking it all in.

I'm alone. That's the first thing I realize as I edge deeper into the room. A trio of windows overlooking the driveway take up one wall, all three of them open to allow cool evening air to drift into the otherwise dusty space. Two easels stand in the center of the room. Canvases are propped along the walls, some of them covered in tarps. A wooden work table rests along the wall closest to the door where cans and tubes of paint are scattered as well as glass jars full of well-worn brushes.

But it's the artwork on the walls that catch my attention. Portraits. Landscapes. Plants and the occasional animal.

And me.

Me looking over my shoulder. Me shirtless, my breasts full and heavy as I look forward with a heated look behind my eyes. Me in the kitchen with a scowl pinching my brows together.

Me smiling up at something unseen, my lips slightly parted.

I slowly turn my attention to the easels and get a closer look at the contents.

Tears spring to my eyes as I gaze at a nearly finished portrait of me laughing, my eyes creased and a startling blue that only someone who's seen me very close up could have captured. Freckles dot the bridge of my nose, and my hair is loose and falling around my sun-kissed shoulders. The colors bleed into a beautiful, rosy background. It's all sunshine and florals and…

I look happy. In most of these portraits I look happy, and if I'm not happy, my eyes are full of unbelievable desire.

I whirl toward a creaking noise behind me. Dalton takes up the entire doorway, his hands tucked casually in the pockets of his jeans, his T-shirt damp with either sweat or rain.

His green eyes meet mine as he closes the door I'd left open, and then we're alone.

"You painted me."

"I said I would."

Charged silence settles between us, broken only by the rising song of the cicadas outside.

"You're not supposed to be here," I say so softly I wonder if he catches it. But, he nods, his mouth parting slightly before he thinks better of saying something and closes them again. I step toward him, my heart and mind at odds, and ask, "Who are you?"

"You know me."

"I barely do," I admit. "I don't even fucking know your last name." I know his body. I know his touch ignites a fire within me that will burn as an ember for the rest of my life. I know his scent. I know how safe I feel in his arms when there's no good reason I should trust him.

Especially now.

He swallows, the column of his throat bobbing with effort as he tears his gaze from my face and looks down at his work table. "It's Rice, and you shouldn't be here, either."

"I was hired–"

"You were hunted," he corrects, his eyes lighting on mine again.

"You need to start explaining what's happening here," I plead, my eyes beginning to water. "I just talked to the lawyer. There's never been boarders here."

"I was given a set of rooms when I was hired as a painter."

"But that was years ago," I whisper. "No one knows you're still here except for me, right? I asked–I asked Bailey about you, and she didn't know who I was talking about. E–Even Vera looked at me like I was speaking in tongues!"

Dalton exhales sharply, his eyes flashing with mingled frustration and annoyance. "I don't know what you want me to say."

"The truth!"

"I was hired five years ago," he grinds out, his jaw sharp and flexed. "I came here just like you did. Bright eyed, excited, thinking that this would be the respite I was looking for after years of fucking *toiling* in New Orleans, fixing up those gaudy mansions, listening to rich wives complain while their husbands carry on with mistresses. I came here because I needed a break, and now I can't leave. Not for long, anyway."

"Why can't you leave?"

He eyes me skeptically, then shakes his head. "It doesn't matter anymore. This has gone way too far."

"What has?"

"This!" He motions to the air between us. "You were never supposed to come here. I knew the second you pulled up that something had gone terribly wrong, and I–I couldn't do anything about it. I couldn't stop any of this from happening. None of it!" He roughly grabs a stool and sits down, running his hands through his hair. Little droplets of rain stick to the silky, dark brown strands. "Vera was in on it. Bringing you here as a nurse. She has access to the entire Gregory directory–every family member you have, old and young. You were exactly what he was looking for. Young, inexperienced, gullible. At least, he thought so." He takes a breath but keeps his head in his hands. "God, Layla, I am so sorry."

"Who are you talking about?"

He looks up at me then. "Asmodeus… Amos."

The name whispers through the air between us on a cold breeze that seems misplaced. It's stiflingly hot tonight, even though all the windows are open, yet my skin prickles with a chill that goes straight to my bones.

"I've heard Aunt Penny say that name–"

"That name," he says, standing, "is the name of an entity. A thing that haunts this house. A name for the demon your family summoned over two centuries ago, Layla. And he's here, now, stuck in this house, delighting in the torture and undoing of everyone he can get his hands on."

"Stop," I tell him, holding my hands out as he approaches me. "This is insane, Dalton."

"You've heard the stories from Curtis. The family deaths. Your aunt's father was killed, and her mother went insane, just like every man and woman who came after. Robert Wilson was telling the truth about those two men who were murdered here. He told the truth about the women they were connected to, as well. And that man you found in the wall–"

"Stop, please!"

"I knew him," he says in such a strained voice it cuts me to my core. "I knew her, too."

"The other night nurse." It's not a question.

The pieces start falling into place as he continues, "They loved each other. Like, true, undying love. He came to visit her here a few weeks before she... left. Everything was fine for the first couple of days, but then they started having dreams."

I close my eyes.

"That's how it starts."

I hear him beginning to pace.

"Dreams—vivid ones. The kind that blur the line between imagination and reality. She'd wake up screaming. He'd try to comfort her, but the dreams were about him doing unimaginable things to her. Raping her, torturing her...."

I find it impossible to breathe.

"She started to turn on him, and at the same time, he was fighting his own mental breakdown. Amos was in his head, too, toying with his reality, chipping away at his psyche until he could get into that man's mind and break him completely. That's how he does it, Layla. He feeds on all of us. He thrives on our fear. It makes him stronger."

I shake my head, choking down a sob.

"He can make himself seem almost human now. It didn't used to be like this. The last night nurse was the tipping point, I believe, based on what I've been able to find out about this kind of...entity."

"I can't–"

"You have to believe me," he says sternly, his eyes meeting mine as he comes to stop a few feet away from me.

"I don't know what to believe!"

"Dr. Ashford!" he shouts. "Do you think that man had the strength, let alone desire, to assault you in the middle of the living room? A man his age shouldn't have been able to overpower someone like you–someone whose dealt with unruly patients, whose had to lift people out of beds–"

"You're saying he was possessed?"

"Yes, Layla."

"This is ridiculous."

"Vera," he says sharply, cutting me off. "Vera is in on this. She's working with him, or he's in her head. He can influence people, especially weak-minded individuals who are more susceptible."

"Do you realize how crazy you sound?"

"Did you not find it odd that a random lawyer in fucking Hahnville reached out to you for a job nursing a sick old woman?"

"I'm her family."

"You," he laughs bitterly, shaking his head, "are being set up to inherit everything. Vera will see to it. That's one of her assignments from him, I'm sure."

My blood runs cold. "What? No. Dalton, I barely know this woman. The house is going to the historical society. We're not close. My family–"

"Penny Gregory is the only one that can keep Amos in check. It's something about your bloodline. Someone summoned him centuries ago, someone in your family, and he's tethered to the heir to this estate. That's why she refused to marry. That's why she refused to have children and why she won't willingly leave the house to you—or anyone in the family." His voice drops low, his eyes going dark.

I shake my head, but what he's saying makes sense.

"That's why Vera keeps her fully sedated and unaware of what's happening. It's so he can remain unchecked. But Penny is weakening. She's old and frail. Vera's interference has caused her health to plummet. If she dies, Amos won't have another heir to cling to. He'll have to start all over again. He's probably afraid he'll return to being a whisper of a spirit in the marsh where someone in your family summoned him centuries ago. That's why you were brought here. That's why he has Vera slowly killing your aunt while he tries to get into your mind. You will be the next Gregory heir, and he'll be able to continue his reign of terror. This house, this fucking property, is tied to all of it. He doesn't want to start over again."

He steps closer to me. I don't back away.

"He had Vera bring you here after running through his last couple. He sent the last night nurse into a state of insanity, burning through her mind. Now he wants you. He needs you. He needs you to submit to him, to be his pet, to allow him the freedoms Penny denied him."

The word "pet" echoes through my head like a death knell.

"What about you, Dalton? If this is true, what do you have to do with it?"

29

DALTON

I SEALED my fate by telling her this. I can feel the shadows beginning to crowd the room as I step toward her, reaching out to her, looking at her for what could be the last time.

I made a deal with the devil in her name. I signed it with blood. I was tricked. I failed to protect her.

I knew Vera would do this. Her plan was already in action years ago before I was hired to start bringing this hellhole back to life–a life Amos was desperate for. He wanted to see the return of the golden age of the property, when parties raged, and there were plenty of minds for him to plunder and the promise of further generations to keep fueling his fire.

Layla, a young, impressionable nursing student, stood out to Amos. She has no idea he's been stalking her from afar for years now, biding his time. Why he waited to try to get into her head until now, I'm not sure, but I imagine it had something to do with the way Penny fought to stay above water and not end up buried in the family cemetery while this demon sinks his claws into fresh blood to ensure several more decades of feeding off the innocent.

"He tried," I say to Layla. "He tried to take over my mind. I came here on the heels of my dad's cancer diagnosis. My dad was supposed to be the one taking this job, not me. I figured out what Amos was early on." I tell her about some of my experiences in other houses and other jobs, where I came into contact with all kinds of things I couldn't explain. Some people are more sensitive to this kind of thing, even if I'd never admit it outwardly.

I saw Amos when he thought I couldn't see him. I could feel him whispering in my ear, feel him trying to claw his way into my mind through the dreams he sent me.

When he couldn't get to me, he let me see him for what he truly was, and at that point, there was no escaping him.

"When I left, he came with me. He can do that for short bursts of time. The bastard tormented my dad. He wanted me to return to this house. He wasn't done with me. I was the only one who'd slipped through his fingers, and he hated it, obsessed over it. I had to come back to keep him from further harming my father. I could have walked away when my dad died two years ago, but then the ball was in motion to get you here somehow. I got whispers of it in my dreams. He wanted you, Layla. He wanted you more than he'd ever wanted anything before. You were his meal ticket for another life-time, and I…" I meet her eyes, finding them misty, but understanding. "I couldn't let him do it."

"You stayed here because of me? But you didn't even know me."

"I did my best to delay him, but when he finally got you here, I tried to get you to leave before he had a chance to start fucking with you," I admit. "I tried to scare you, to drive you out. When that didn't work, and you started having dreams…." I let my own desires get in the way. I wanted her as badly as he did, maybe more. "He thought he'd finally beaten me. That I was playing into his sick little games with you. That you and I were forming a connection he could use to turn you against me when the time was right. He believed you'd kill me if he pushed you hard enough, scared you enough, made you distrustful but you–you didn't."

She submitted to me. She took me as I was. She wanted me, not him, and she eventually saw past his bullshit dreams. She saw past his manipulation. She was brave. She was hardheaded. She wasn't afraid.

She was like me, the person he hates the most.

"He's going to kill us both," I tell her.

She stares up at me. I wonder how long I've been talking, rambling, honestly. This whole thing is unbelievable, every word of it, but her eyes shine with pain as she reaches up and strokes my cheek then tucks one of my curls behind my ear.

"You've been here alone this whole time? Did Curtis know? Bailey?" she asks.

"Neither of them. Curtis is somehow immune to Amos. I'm not sure why. Amos doesn't see him as a threat. He takes care of the house, which in turn, I believe, is like taking care of Amos in a way. Bailey… she's an easy target. I couldn't let her see me. I couldn't give Amos a reason to invade her dreams with my image. She would have been easy to break down if she slept here enough times. She's good, Layla."

"He'll go after her," she says hurriedly, a hint of panic in her voice. "Oh, God, Dalton. She stayed the night last night."

"I know."

"She told me she had weird dreams last night."

I nod, a heavy weight settling in the pit of my stomach. It's at the moment I see something shift on the far side of the room. A shadow plays across the wall before disappearing from view. My senses go on high alert when a screeching noise echoes through the house, and then a song plays several levels below us at an impossible loud volume.

"St. James Infirmary."

Layla goes pale. "He–that night…." She stumbles over the words. "I thought it was you. In the foyer. He–he lifted me onto the piano and…oh, God! I thought it was you."

She nearly collapses in my arms. I clutch her to me, the hair on the back of my neck standing on end as the energy in the house shifts to something charged and dangerous.

He's here now. I can feel him. I can sense him trying to shove his way into my head, to take over like he's been trying to for years.

He's desperate now. He's been pushing us both to the edge for the past few weeks. "Layla," I whisper over the booming music. "Look at me, Angel."

She does, her eyes shining with tears and terror.

"Whatever happens next, I need you to know that I—everything I did was for you. I tried, Layla. I tried to keep you out of this. He wants me dead and out of his way as much as he wants you to submit to him. I need you to leave this place and get as far away as you can, right now."

She clutches my shirt. "Dalton, no."

"Take your aunt and go. Can you get her down the stairs and into your car?"

"Maybe, but—"

"You have to leave. He won't follow you if I'm still here. He can't leave this place for long because of the spell. Besides, this is between me and him now. He's been using my image to torment you, to haunt you. I don't know how much longer I can keep him from—"

Pain shoots through the back of my head, something sharp and deadly. It cuts me off, and the second I close my eyes against the agony there, I feel him clawing into my subconscious. "You need to leave, now! Get your aunt out of the house. Get her off the property. I think—I think I can end this."

"I'm not going without you!"

It takes all of my strength, but I push her up against my work table. "Listen to everything I say, all right? You are mine. You've been mine since the beginning. You will be mine tonight, and when the sun rises tomorrow, even if I'm gone, you'll still be mine. He cannot have you. I will gladly die knowing I'm dragging him to hell with me."

"What are you going to do?"

I take her face between my hands and kiss her soundly, roughly parting her lips with my tongue. She moans, gathering me close, and then I'm standing between her knees while she yanks at my belt, pulling it free from my jeans.

"You're mine!" she shouts against my lips, her voice strained and full of hurt. "Dalton, please!"

This is the last time I'll see her. The last time I'll taste her on my tongue. The last time her soft voice will fill my ears, and her scent will wrap around me.

All of this has been worth it since it meant I got a few weeks with her.

I cup the back of her head and kiss her like my life depends on it–because maybe it does. Amos is raging now. I can hear glass shattering downstairs, several stories below. Layla must hear it too because she chokes out a sob and grinds her hips into mine. "P-Please, Dalton?"

Fear turns her on. She's as dark and twisted as I am. It's why she's lasted this long.

I reach between us and pull her panties to the side, then bury my cock deep inside her pussy. I claim her with each brutal thrust, the table slamming into the wall, cutting through the music seeping through every crack in the floorboards. I hold her close, whispering praise in her ear, over her skin, until I feel her muscles clamping down around my cock.

"You've been such a good girl," I tell her. "My Angel. Always, my Angel."

She tangles her fingers in my hair and pulls me down so I'm caging her in against the table's surface. Cans of paint fall to the floor all around us, splattering over the floorboards.

We ignore Amos. I ignore his raged attempts at breaking into my head as I drown myself in Layla and keep her at the forefront of my mind.

It's so unfair that we don't have more time. I could have married this girl. I could have the kind of life I'd thought I'd given up years ago with her by my side.

And because of that, I'll do whatever it takes to send this beast back to hell so that she, at least, has a chance for the kind of life she deserves.

"D-Dalton," she whimpers, her skin suddenly going frigid with chills.

"Eyes on me," I rasp, knowing exactly why she's suddenly going rigid to the touch. He's here. Behind us. Watching us fuck like animals. He's watching us–knowing she knows the truth, and that he'll never have her.

I won.

After all of this time, I won.

Her climax rips through her, shaking me to my core. Her pussy spasms, the feeling leaving me breathless as I bury myself to the hilt and come hard, keeping her locked in place.

I haven't even pulled out when I whisper in her ear, "Go."

I look her in the eyes as I slowly pull out. They're beautiful, but determined.

"I trust you," she whispers against my lips, and then she's gone.

30

LAYLA

I DON'T LOOK behind me as I run out of Dalton's studio. Whatever was in the room with us–I don't want to see it. The feeling of it watching me—watching us–still drifts over my skin as I grab the banister and slide down the stairs, nearly falling all the way down in my haste to get to Aunt Penny's room.

I can't hear myself think over the blaring music. The song plays over, and over, and over, the screeching of the ancient record sending shockwaves through the house.

But I know one thing is true. Dalton isn't lying. I believe everything he told me. It's unbelievable, but so is everything that's happened to me since I arrived at this place, and Dalton has been the only real, tangible thing keeping me grounded.

There has to be a way out of this for both of us.

I yank Penny's door open and fly into the room.

"It's too late," she says, and I feel my body go numb in shock.

Penny is standing near an open window dressed in a white night-gown, her rail-thin figure silhouetted by the shadow of the moon peeking through the storm clouds. She looks over her shoulder at me, a somber smile touching her lips. "Poor thing. I tried to stop this from happening. Years ago, I thought depriving myself of a husband and children would bring an end to this madness. Amos is a tricky bastard. I tried to find a way to banish him, you know. That's how all of this started–the medications, the sedation.… He knew I was looking for a way to banish him back to the same ether our family pulled him from all those centuries ago. My great-great-grandmother wanted more. More money, more luck, more power. That's how he came here. She called to him, summoned him, using dark magic, I'm sure"

I shake the shock from my mind and shout, "What can we do?"

She turns halfway to face me, holding a lit candle in her hands. I can't even think about how she got her hands on matches at the moment. "There's nothing to do. As long as this cursed house stands, he has a place to conduct his evil deeds. He's so strong now. I should have known he'd find a way to stop me. He was nothing more than a whisper when I was young, but now?"

A crash sounds overhead. My heart nearly stops. "Dalton?"

"Poor boy," she says, clicking her tongue. "He loves you dearly, you know."

"How do you know about him?"

"I am still in here, girl, usually locked away in my mind. But I knew all that happens in this house. Dalton checks on me every night, you know. He sits here sometimes and talks to me. Talks to me about you, and how hard he's trying to get you out. I didn't have the strength to tell him it was too late. But now… I underestimated you. You're like me. You saw past Amos and his tricks. You tethered your-self to something real, something rare."

"What's that?"

"Love," she says wistfully, smiling to herself.

My heart is in my throat as she starts turning to the window. "We have to leave, Aunt Penny."

She sighs, shaking her head. "No. I'm going to stay."

"You can't. It's not safe."

The music suddenly stops. Bailey's voice cuts through the air in concern. "Layla?"

"Oh, no," I practically screech. Why is she here? I look between Aunt Penny and the door, my heart twisting.

Aunt Penny just looks at me with a sad smile on her face and nods.

"Stay here," I command, then race out of the room and into the hallway. Bailey is running up the stairs, panting, her eyes wide with shock.

"What the hell is going on? I turned off that music--"

"Get out, now! Go back to your car!"

"I forgot my phone charger in your room." Another crash sounds overhead. "What the fuck is happening?"

I grab her shoulders, shaking her, but then I smell smoke. "Nooo!" I groan, my voice pitched as I whirl back toward Aunt Penny's room. I try shoving Bailey back down the stairs, but she pushes past me.

We sprint into Penny's room just in time to witness the curtains erupting in flames, the heat fanning over the wallpaper, causing it to wither and catch fire as if she's used some accelerant. But then, this is an old house, and the walls are like kindling.

Penny stands with her back to it all, her eyes locked on mine.

"Ms. Penny!" Bailey shouts, lunging for her.

"Get her out!" I scream. "We have to get her out!"

We take Penny by the arms and drag her out of her room. She fights us the whole way, kicking and screaming, but she's weak from age and years spent in bed.

"Let it burn! Let it burn to the ground! *Let it burn!*" she screams. "Leave me here to burn with it!"

Smoke chokes out the air in the hallway as we rush down the stairs. "It's the only way!"

But at the front door, I shove Penny into Bailey's arms. "Take her to the Wilsons' house. Call the fire department."

Bailey nods, her eyes wide as I turn back to the staircase. "What the hell are you doing, Layla?"

"I have to go back for him."

"For who?" she pleads, tears springing to life along her lashes.

"He's gone, girl," Penny says, her voice low and full of warning. "The man you love is no longer there. He took over. He'll try to fool you–"

"What are you both talking about, Layla?"

"He gave you this chance. Don't waste it!"

"I have to save him. I can't let him die!"

The fire has breached the entire second level. It roars with each inch of the house it consumes. Bailey edges toward the door, still hoping I'm coming with her.

"Layla, no!"

I sprint away, down the hallway to the kitchen.

She'll get Penny out of the house. I know she will. I have to believe Bailey will save Aunt Penny and my choices right now won't be in vain.

Because I'm not leaving this fucking place without Dalton.

I pull a knife from the drawer near the sink, catching my reflection in the polished steel… and his reflection, staring right back at me from over my shoulder.

I turn to face him. "Let's go, Dalton."

He shrugs, completely casual despite the fact the house is burning down around us. "What's the rush?"

I look into his cold, lifeless eyes. They're still that beautiful, jade green I love, but somehow changed. He steps closer to me, close enough to touch. I reach out and push a finger into his chest.

He feels real.

I yank my hand back right as he goes to grab my wrist.

"Don't be like that," he says smoothly.

"We need to leave."

"And then what, Layla?" He laughs, and it's a menacing sound I've never heard from him before. I know it's not him. Maybe it's his body, maybe not, but that thing–Amos–took over just like Dalton said he would. Still, it's difficult to keep my wits about me as he steps closer, and I keep stepping back until my hips brush the counter. I sidestep toward the backdoor.

God, the heat is overwhelming. Smoke begins to flood the room. My eyes burn, but I force them open.

"You tell me," I croak. The room is nearly airless now. I need to get out. I need to get Dalton out somehow.

"Did you really think I wanted anything from you? You were just a body to fuck, Layla. I never loved you."

"Dalton, we're going to die in here!"

"Good. Your death wouldn't be that much of a loss, would it? You've always been such a disappointment, haven't you? You've never truly been happy. You spent years going from one place to another, looking for connections, running from your family and its history…. But look at you now. You came crawling back here, to where it all started, didn't you?"

"Dalton!" I shout. "We need to leave. I'm not leaving without you!"

His eyes suddenly clear, a shred of the real Dalton gleaming there for a fraction of a second, and I know I have to save him—his body. He pitches forward, his hand to his chest. The moment passes as quickly as it came, and then Amos is back.

"Come here, Layla."

"No." I stand my ground, digging in my heels. "We're leaving."

"You're not going anywhere."

"Wanna fucking bet?"

His lips curl over his top teeth in a wholly demonic smile, and then I'm running as fast as I can. He lunges for me, but I duck out of the way. His clumsy body slams into the kitchen table. It's so strange, the way he moves now. Like this demon isn't sure how to handle possessing a human body in full, his energy trying to take up every piece of Dalton and bend it to his will. Or, I hope, it's Dalton fighting back as he chases me down the hallway toward the front foyer.

The stairwell is totally engulfed in flames. I race toward the front door, wanting to lead him out of the house and into the driveway, out of harm's way.

But he grabs my hair and yanks me down, slamming my body into the ground. The knife slides across the floor, just out of reach.

"Stupid little pet," he drawls, straddling me. I reach for the knife, screaming with the effort as my fingers graze the sharp edge of the blade. "I do love how you struggle."

The ceiling in the living room beside us begins to cave in, sending embers and active flames crashing to the floor, igniting the furniture. The grand piano groans as fire licks up its sides.

"D-Dalton!" I scream, my fingers dancing over the knife. Just a little bit more–a little further–and my fingers will be on it.

His hand wraps around my throat and squeezes hard enough to make my vision go blurry. There's no air. I can't force oxygen into my lungs. The fire is creeping closer, mere yards away.

"D-D-Dalton!" I wheeze, just as my fingertips find grip on the blade and arch, pulling it just a fraction of an inch toward where I'm lying, where I'm dying.

"We could have ruled together," he whispers. "You could have been my queen."

"Fuck you," I whimper, my lungs screaming for air.

I'm going to die. I can feel it. I can feel death already snaking through my veins. I use the last of my strength to grip the blade, and then I swing, closing my eyes and whispering, "I'm so sorry. I'm so, so sorry."

Dalton sacrificed himself to allow me a way out.

He should have known I wouldn't have gone without him.

The knife hits something soft, then hard, flesh giving way to bone.

An unearthly scream pierces the air as my vision goes completely black and raw, scorching heat fans over my body. The scream continues for what feels like eternity, and maybe it is eternity. I've never experienced death. I've seen it countless times, but I was always an onlooker, the witness.

I hear what sounds like a train ripping through the house as the fire consumes the first floor, taking me and Dalton with it.

31

LAYLA

DEATH IS COLD AND EMPTY. It's silent. It's lonely.

I feel weightless, like I'm being carried. But there's no sound, no feeling in my body. Just a faint, flashing light.

Everyone talks about seeing a light at the end of the tunnel. Follow the light--into death.

Whenever people talk of the light they follow into heaven—or in my case, it's probably hell—I always imagined it would be bright white.

Not flashing red and blue like this light.

"Come on, darling. That's it, now. Breathe deep."

Air fills my lungs–cool and rich, and my body explodes back to life. My eyes fly open, the flashing lights of half a dozen police and fire vehicles filling the space all around me, blurring my senses.

"Big breath for me now," Robert Wilson says, one of his hands cupping the back of my head as the other keeps an oxygen mask fastened to my nose and mouth. "Come on, Layla. Another breath. Big breath this time."

I suck in, my eyes going wider as my senses creep back to life.

Robert's eyes crease with joy and relief. He turns his face toward someone nearby, his voice unintelligible as it bleeds with the sounds of sirens and rushing water. I painfully turn my head to the side. The house comes into view–or what's left of it. The fire continues to burn despite the firefighters. The upper levels have caved in on the first floor. Heat wafts toward me, stinging my eyes.

A familiar muffled voice nearby catches my attention, and I crane my neck toward the sound. It's Bailey, wrapped in a blanket and sitting in the bed of a pickup truck stamped with "Hahnville Fire Chief" on the side. A gorgeous man fully decked out in fire gear talks to her as she sips from a water bottle, her eyes misted with shocked tears.

I shove Robert and the oxygen mask away, coming to my senses fully. "Aunt Penny?"

"She's fine," Robert says, securing the mask to my face again. "Everybody's fine. Bailey drove like a bat out of hell to my place. Penny is with Helen, and the police chief right now, back at my house."

"How–how did I–"

"You'll never believe it," he laughs heartily. "Remember the day we came to meet you, and we talked in the dining room about the wallpaper? An artist came down from New Orleans for the job some time ago. I guess he came back tonight to start on one of the other rooms."

"What?"

"He pulled you out. I got here just as the fire department came blaring down the driveway. That man walking out on the porch with you in his arms was quite a sight, I'll tell you what."

"Where is he?" Hope, and terror, nearly stop my heart.

I'd stabbed him. I'd stabbed Dalton, knowing I'd die in the fire. I couldn't let Amos have him, even if it meant taking him into death with me.

Maybe that's what all of these women were doing all along. Maybe they knew about Amos, and he gave them no choice but to kill the men they loved to try to rid them of the demon that took over their bodies.

"He's getting patched up right now by the medics. We got an ambulance coming for you, don't worry."

"I don't need it. Where is he? Please?"

"He got stabbed in the arm by some debris on his way out of the house I heard. Don't worry about it now."

In the arm? Had my aim been so poor? I had been suffocating.

"Why is Bailey here?" My head feels heavy.

"She basically dumped Ms. Penny in our driveway and screamed at us to call the fire department before hauling ass over here again. I guess she went in after you but got knocked off her feet by a wall of fire. Tanner, the fire chief, is taking care of her while his boys try to put out the fire…" he tapers off. "Listen, darling. The house is a total loss."

Thank God.

"Ms. Penny, however, was the most lucid I've ever seen. Real apologetic, too. Said she lit a candle and walked to the window to look outside at the moon. Her eyes aren't working too well these days, you know, thought the candle would help her see what she wanted to see but she lit her old lace curtains on fire instead."

A delirious laugh works its way up my throat. Robert smiles down at me, concern showing clearly on his face.

"That's… that's a shame." I want to say something else—that it's glorious. Now, Amos will have nowhere to do his bidding. We've won.

Overhead, the night sky gives way to the first hints of morning, the clouds parting enough to see the faint outline of the stars as the sky goes from an inky black to deep violet.

I look up at the stars, tears rolling down my cheeks.

And then a shadow passes overhead, blocking my view of the heavens.

Dalton looks down at me as he kneels, his hand warm against my cheek. I realize with a start that I'm lying in the back of one of the volunteer firemen's truck, the metal hard and solid against my spine.

I lock eyes with Dalton. My chest strains, but I'm unable to breathe.

Is this Dalton?

Or Amos?

"Angel," he whispers, his voice ragged and choked.

"Well, I'd say you were her guardian angel tonight, sir. You got here just in the nick of time."

"I've got it from here. The ambulance is on its way down the driveway, finally," Dalton says softly, not providing any more explanation to Robert. His eyes don't leave mine for a single second. Robert moves away with a nod, giving us a moment.

I reach up and grip his wrist, finding it warm to the touch. His clothes are scorched and hanging off his body, and his back is covered by another one of those shiny silver blankets like Bailey's.

"Is this real?" I ask as he removes the oxygen mask from my face and leans down. "Are you here?"

"You did it, Angel."

I close my eyes as his lips brush mine, tasting of ash and salt. Warmth spreads through me, waking up the numb parts of my body as I slowly crawl back to life.

It's gone.

The fire spread to the garage and outbuildings despite the fire department's best efforts. Nothing but the foundation remains.

Everything is all black—tendrils of smoke continuing to rise in soft wisps in the warm summer breeze.

My Toyota 4Runner is nothing but a shell of scorched metal.

Everything is gone.

Including Amos.

I watch as Dalton and Curtis walk back toward where I'm standing in the driveway with Bailey. They're taking their time. I wonder what they're talking about.

"He seems nice," Bailey says softly, her arm linked in mine. "You should have told me about him sooner. You didn't need to sneak him into the house, you know."

I shrug, smiling to myself. I lied, of course. What good is the truth now, after everything that happened? To Bailey, I just had a secret lover.

"It's been a while since I had a boyfriend," I admit, because that's definitely the truth.

"Me too," she breathes, chuckling.

It's been three days since the fire. One of those days was spent being poked and prodded at the hospital, and the others were spent shacked up at a bed and breakfast in town with Dalton. We waited for the worst, for Amos to reappear to torment us further, but were met with peace—and time to really get to know each other.

We didn't leave our room for two whole days. We were too busy living, and fucking, of course, without the watchful, vengeful gaze of a demon peering at us from every angle.

"But guess what? I have a date next weekend," Bailey says slyly, giving my shoulder a little nudge.

"With who?"

"The fire chief."

"You dog," I grin, nudging her back.

We smile at each other, then laugh, our joy lifting toward the unrelenting sun.

Curtis calls Bailey over, and I watch as she passes by Dalton, who is on his way over to me. They smile at each other, saying something I can't hear in passing, but Dalton's answering laugh ignites something deep in my heart.

He's been so happy lately. He smiles nonstop. He still fucks me like a god, despite his new disposition. That bitter cold edge to him has loosened, leaving room for *this*.

"Hey," he says before pressing a quick kiss to my lips.

"Hey," I reply as his hand grazes down to the small of my back.

"Ready to get out of here? Curtis is going to drive Bailey over to the Wilsons' for lunch."

"Yeah, we're going to be late if we waste any more time."

He knits his fingers in mine as he walks me back to the SUV we rented since both of our vehicles are now piles of twisted metal.

"It's a pretty nice place," he says over the soft sounds of the radio as we drive across town closer to New Orleans. Eventually, a small hospital comes into view in the distance, gleaming in the sun. "She'll be safe here until she's ready to go to her new place. It's a community, you know. They have their own restaurants, entertainment centers, and nurses on staff twenty-four-seven."

"She showed me the pamphlet this morning," I reply, my face tilted toward the open window. "I feel a little uneasy about sending her all the way to Florida."

"It was her idea, Layla," he laughs, his eyes on the road ahead.

"Still, Florida is far away."

We pull into the parking lot, and Dalton cuts the engine then rests his hands in his lap. "I have a job down in Miami. I confirmed it this morning. I'll be close by. Your aunt won't be alone."

I bite my lip, rolling it between my teeth.

"What if you came with me?" he asks.

I steal a glance at him. "Are you sure?"

"Are you serious, Angel?" He leans toward me, taking my chin between his thumb and forefinger, and plants a kiss to my lips. "I want that more than anything."

I smile, knowing I'll be able to find a job in Florida. There are always older people needing help down there.

We spend the rest of the day with Aunt Penny, who is recuperating at the hospital before she's transferred down to the retirement home of her choosing in Florida, where the sun always shines, and no demons walk the halls of her new home.

If she ever had dementia, no one would be able to tell now. It's like a fog has been lifted all around us, allowing the sun to touch our skin for the first time in weeks, and in her case, years.

Bad things happened in that house. Dark and twisted things. Something imprinted on my heart while I was there.

But it's no longer with me and no longer plagues Aunt Penny—or Dalton.

I turn to him as we walk back out to the car. He stops walking, swirling the keys over his finger.

"I'll go with you," I tell him.

His smile lights up my soul.

I love him. God, I love him.

We drive out of Hahnville that very night, and as I fall asleep with my head lulling against the window, I swear I hear a faint melody playing somewhere far, far away.

"So sweet, so cold, so fair..."

EPILOGUE

JULIA

"It's... Well, uh–"

"Can you imagine it, Julia? The garage will go there, and over here–" He waves his hand to the far side of what looks like it used to be a driveway of some kind, but grass has started spreading through every crack in the concrete. "I'm thinking three, four stories. With a pool, of course."

I cross my arms under my breasts, my heels clacking on the concrete. "I'm not seeing it, Jake."

Jake, my husband, rolls his brown eyes as he turns his back to me and spreads his arms wide. "This is twenty fucking acres, babe. We can't get this in New Orleans."

"I wanted ocean views."

"Then I'll cut down some trees, baby. Hell, the Gulf is right out there." He whirls back to me, giving me that charming, cocky smile that made me fall in love with him three years ago. "I promised I'd build your dream house, didn't I?"

"My dream," I remind him as he nuzzles my neck, "was a pristine, white mansion on the beach."

"I'll build you another one then," he laughs. "I'll build you three mansions."

"Fine, but I get to pick out the paint and flooring."

"Oh, of course."

He wraps his arms around my waist, but the sound of a large vehicle bumping down the severely overgrown driveway catches our attention.

I smooth the fabric of my tight white sundress and push my Gucci sunglasses up the bridge of my nose. "What the hell is the fire chief doing here?"

"He's the volunteer fire chief, Julia. He's also our contractor," Jake says, running his fingers through his hair, his gold Rolex gleaming in the sun. "Listen, babe. I got a screaming deal on this property. Pennies compared to what it's worth. We're gonna build this house, and if you don't love it, we'll sell it for millions. I'll buy you a fucking island in the Caribbean after this with the money I'm going to make. Just wait and see."

I hum my approval. Jake is good with money. He can turn a penny into a million dollars in a blink.

Still, this place gives me the creeps.

I frown at the shaded groves of trees choked with vines that surround the cleared center of the property.

The fire chief, who is a lot younger and far more handsome than I envisioned, steps out of his truck and starts talking to Jake.

Bored, I start walking, acting like I'm entirely invested in this place and find every blade of grass interesting. I hear them talking, but I'm not paying attention. I lift my head and peer out in the distance, trying to see the Gulf.

I see something else instead.

"Is that a fucking cemetery?" I almost squeal before scoffing, and turning my back to the headstones rising in the distance. "Jesus Christ."

"Julia, come over here and meet Tanner Hendricks." Jake waves me over, and I reluctantly obey, casting a glance over my shoulder at the creepy cemetery and the standing water all around it. We'll have to do something about that.

Tanner is tall with dark brown hair and a ruggedly handsome face. He looks like he chops wood and drinks straight whiskey. He probably wears flannel and has a Labrador, too.

"You must be a busy man," I drawl, shaking his hand. "Fire chief, contractor, and… what else?"

"Just that, ma'am," he says with a smile. "The fire department is volunteer, so I have to make a living somehow."

"Speaking of fire," Jake says, "The old house burned down, right?"

"Yeah, you're right. Last summer."

"I've seen pictures of the original house," Jakes says, blowing out his breath. "What a loss."

"Yeah, well, no one was more disappointed than the historical society. They were supposed to get the house when the last Gregory died. The family has owned this place for as long as anyone can remember. You're the second owner in its entire history."

"Lucky us," I say sarcastically.

Jake shoots me a look then asks, "Why did the previous owner sell so cheap? Nobody's been able to tell me that, but seeing as you're local–"

"Penny Gregory passed away a few months ago. The land went to historical society, who see no need for it now that the house is gone. Her distant relatives didn't want the property, so they sold it."

"Is that who we contact about the cemetery?" I ask.

"If you want to know about who's buried there, the local archives–"

"To remove it," I correct.

Tanner gives me an odd look, but Jake cuts in. "Let's get down to business, shall we? I have a few things I want to run by you…"

Jake leads him away, leaving me in the center of the decaying driveway. I huff out an annoyed breath and pull my phone out of my purse. I barely have service. Is Jake really serious about this place?

I turn back to the marsh beyond the overgrown patch of flat land where the house used to sit. We're supposed to be building a house to raise our future family in.

This isn't what I envisioned.

I squint into the glare of the sun. Did I just see a man standing in the cemetery?

∼

Tanner

I UNLOCK my front door and walk inside my craftsman style house in the outskirts of Hahnville. It's quiet. It usually is when Bailey isn't home. She works three-twelves in New Orleans right now, and won't be home until sometime tomorrow.

When she's not in NOLA, she's been staying here lately. I like having her around. We haven't officially moved in together yet. I should ask her formally, I think. I should get down on one knee for that girl, honestly.

I should spread her legs and nibble down her inner thighs, then swipe my tongue through her folds until she squirms and starts begging for more.

"Christ," I say out loud, scratching my head before running my hand down my face. I don't know where those dominant thoughts came from, but my balls are tight and my cock is aching against my jeans.

I try to ignore the image of Bailey sprawled out beneath me, my hand squeezing her neck while she spasms around my cock. We've had sex lots of times, but we've never done anything like that.

I sit down at my desk in the living room, blinking to clear my mind as I boot up my computer and try to get some work done.

The couple who bought the old Gregory property are from Texas, apparently. They have big dreams for the massive mansion they're wanting to build, but the wife isn't so sure about the property itself.

I don't blame her.

That place has always given me the creeps.

The fire last year had been a brutal reminder of how quickly these old plantation homes can wither to ash and dust. The Gregory estate was one of only a handful left.

Now, it will be a massive modern house with gold finishes.

My mind drifts back to the night of the fire as I go through blueprints. I get a text from one of my guys at the station just checking in. It's a quiet night. No fires to put out, no car accidents. No need for me, at least not yet.

I have all night to start implementing the changes Jake wanted to see, but I find it hard to focus. Bailey keeps crowding my mind.

I get up an hour later to pour myself a drink. The house is too quiet without her laughter, so I hook up my phone to my Bluetooth speaker and put my music library on shuffle.

A song I don't think I've ever heard before starts to play. I like the sound of it, but I don't know where it came from. I look down at my phone. I must have added it to this playlist by accident at some point.

I tuck my phone in my pocket and sip my drink, leaning on the archway leading into the kitchen as I listen to the lyrics.

Bailey creeps back into my mind–naked, and looking over her shoulder. She beckons to me, her lips parted in a sly smile.

"Claim her," comes a whispered voice from everywhere, and nowhere.

I blink. The vision of my girlfriend shatters, and I find myself alone again.

"Folks, I'm going down to St. James Infirmary–see my baby there. She's laid out on a long white table. So sweet, so cold, so fair."

ALSO BY BELLA MOONDRAGON

One Night with the Billionaire

Shared by the Sexy Billionaire Twins

The Alpha King's Breeder series:

Bought by the Alpha: The Alpha King's Breeder Book 1

Loved by the Alpha: The Alpha King's Breeder Book 2

Lost by the Alpha: The Alpha King's Breeder Book 3

Luna of the Alpha: The Alpha King's Breeder Book 4

Legacy of the Alpha: The Alpha Kings's Breeder Book 5

Daughter of the Alpha: The Alpha King's Breeder Book 6

Descendants of the Alpha: The Alpha King's Breeder Book 7

Shadow of the Alpha: The Alpha King's Breeder Book 8

Son of the Alpha: The Alpha King's Breeder Book 9

The Luna's Vampire Prince series:

The Culling

The Kingdom

The Conquered

Pregnant With Four Alphas' Babies

Chosen As the Breeder

Mated to Four Alphas

Threats Against the Breeder

At War for the Breeder

The Stolen Breeder

Four Alphas, Four Babies

Becoming the Luna Queen

Descendants of the Breeder (releases 9/1/2024)

Desired by the Devil series

Whispers of the Devil

Banter of the Devil (coming soon)

The Mafia Kings series

Indebted to the Mafia King

<u>Loved by the Mafia King</u>

Sign up for Bella's newsletter here.

Follow Bella on Facebook here.